TEMPEST

by

Susan Elle

For

Ursula Publishing UK

TEMPEST
Text Copyright © 2013
by Susan Elle
Ursula Publishing UK
All Rights Reserved

Cover Photograph
© Slavik65 | Dreamstime.com

ISBN 978-1-910753-03-3

Other Books by Susan Elle

The Sara Colson Trilogy includes
Sara's Child
Sara's Loss
Sara's Shame
All the above also available as audio books.

Catherine Colson-Sayers Investigations
CCS Investigations : Bk 1 : Missing
CCS Investigations : Bk 2 : The Chosen
CCS Investigations : Bk 3 : Travis
CCS Investigations : Bk 4 : Deleted
CCS Investigations : Bk 5 : Mind Games, due out end
Aug 2015, twice the length of previous books.

Tempest
Broken

Love, Lies & Consequences Trilogy
Love : Bk1
Lies : Bk2
Consequences : Bk3

Langdon Trilogy
Heart & Home : Bk1
Heart of a Lion : Bk2
Heart of Stone : Bk3
www.susan-elle.com

Table of Contents

<u>PROLOGUE</u>

Shenna pulls into a parking space having driven on auto-pilot since she got the call on her mobile telling her that her husband has taken a turn for the worse.

If the car is locked then that had been done on auto-pilot too - Shenna doesn't know anything other than the fact that Cade needs her, she just has to be in time.

Her feet have wings - she rounds the corner into the lift lobby and can see people waiting for the lifts to arrive. Veering off, Shenna takes the stairs even though Haematology is on the third floor. By the time she reaches the ward she is panting and trembling.

"It's alright, Mrs Williams," a kindly nurse that Shenna has come to know over the last weeks smiles her calming welcome and guides Shenna to a chair.

"I should get in there…see Cade…I need to tell him…I…" Shenna's voice fades away becoming as small as she feels she is becoming.

Her wonderful husband, the man she loves with all her heart, is dying and there is nothing she can do to stop it from happening.

"Just take a breath, Mrs Williams, you look ready to collapse yourself," the nurse observes, frowning at her gaunt face and soft green eyes that seem impossibly large and desperate. Looking up she nods at a nurse that has just exited Cade's room and who signals to her that everything is ready. "Ok now, we've finished giving your husband a freshen-up and a shave," she smiles at Shenna, a warm sympathetic but encouraging smile. "He didn't want you to see him 'in the rough' he called it," and Shenna actually manages a shaky laugh.

"That's what he always calls it when he hasn't shaved," Shenna nods, "he hates going without a shave."

Getting to their feet, Shenna and the nurse walk over to Cade's door. "He's alright, Shenna, we've increased the Morphine so that he isn't in too much pain, but not enough to make him sleepy." Giving Shenna's arm a supportive squeeze, the nurse walks back to the nurses' station and swallows back the tears that have balled up in her throat.

Shenna gives herself a mental shake and stiffens her spine. By the time she sits at Cade's bedside her lips are wearing a convincing smile and her eyes are warm with love.

"Wow, you look as handsome as the day I met and drooled all over you at uni'," she tells him and leans over to kiss his smiling lips.

They were holding hands and he gave hers a squeeze. "And you look every bit as beautiful as the day I first laid eyes on you - the day I tripped over my own tongue and my heart landed right at your feet." His smile lights his eyes with remembering. "Love at first sight - I never believed in it until I saw you, then every other woman just faded away, I only ever had eyes for you, Shenna."

"Ditto," she tells him and draws his hand up to her lips.

"You'll be alright, Shenna...I've made sure you won't struggle financially...no listen...," he tells her when Shenna frowns and shakes her head, "...it's important to me that I at least take care of your financial future - I just wish I could have taken care of you in every other way, too, but it's out of both our hands now."

Laying her head on his arm, Shenna has to fight back the tears that are threatening and the anger that has been growing in her every day since they found out about the cancer.

"I know, Cade," her hand still in his she turns her face to the side to kiss his arm, "I'm just being selfish and thoughtless - I'm sorry."

His other hand reaches over to stroke her hair. "You don't have a selfish bone in your body," he tells her and places a tender kiss on her hair. "Now climb up here and lay with me, I want to feel you in my arms for a while."

Lifting her head to look at him, Shenna eye's the IV line attached to his arm. She wants to be held by him, too, but she doesn't want to disrupt the source of his pain relief.

Following her gaze, Cade smiles encouragingly. "It's taped in good and secure - you won't hurt me, Shenna - just lay with me a while."

Doing as he asks, Shenna carefully lies down on the bed and feels his arms tighten around her. They lack the strength they once had, but hold her with all the love they ever did.

"I love you so much, Cade," Shenna tightens her hold on her husband. "I have something I need to tell you, only I don't know if it will please you or make the parting harder." *And I can't bear to hurt you, not ever, but especially not now.*

His hand stills the stroking of her hair and lifts her chin so that he can see her troubled face. "Just tell me, Shenna, the parting is going to be hard no matter what."

Closing her eyes she hopes her news will give him some joy in his last hours and not add to the pain. "I'm pregnant, Cade - we're going to have a baby."

At first she feels him go perfectly still then his arms tighten around her. "A baby…are you sure?" He feels her nod against his chest and the brightest smile spreads across his amazed face and shines in his tear filled eyes. "A baby! Have you thought of any names?"

He sounds happy…*but is that for me or is he really as overjoyed as he sounds?* "I thought it might be nice to name a boy after his daddy, Cade junior," she tells him wistfully.

But Cade frowns and shakes his head. "No, Shenna, don't put that burden on the boy," he tells her softly. "He doesn't need the fact that he doesn't have a father rubbing in every time anyone uses his name."

"I never thought of it like that," and raises her head up to look at him. "What would you like him to be called?"

He considers, then smiles broadly. "Neirin, it's a sturdy Welsh name meaning 'modest' and 'noble' and my grandfather wore it well."

Shenna returns his smile and nods in approval. "Neirin it is...," she agrees, "...I always loved your granddad, and you're right, he wore his name well."

They lay quiet, each mulling over their own thoughts.

"So...what if it's a girl?" she shifts to look at him again. "Do you have a preference?"

"Well...I've always liked my mother's name, Nareene," Cade looks wistful as he thinks of her, "it means 'contented', and as long as she's tending her family that's just what she is."

Laying her head back down on his chest she smiles into him. "That's settled then - Neirin for a boy and Nareene for a girl."

Just that little conversation seems to have worn him out. Shenna can feel his breathing even out and shallow and knows that Cade has fallen asleep.

CHAPTER ONE

The Iceni Forest is cold and wearing a jacket of snow. The river that runs through it is more of a stream most of the time and is frozen over too.

"Come on, Neirin, if you don't get your skates on we won't have time for a walk," standing with hands on hips, Shenna shouts up the stairs to her four year old son.

"I'm coming," Neirin rounds the top of the stairs with the scarf he's been looking for hanging around his shoulders. Holding tight to the handrail, as his mother taught him, he makes his way down the stairs and grins up at Shenna.

Her heart melts and her snippiness evaporates. "Here now, let me put that on properly so you'll be warm enough." She wraps the scarf a couple of times around his neck then tucks both ends into his coat and fastens the top button over it. "Ok, you look warm enough," Shenna nods with satisfaction as she pulls his woolly hat over his ears. "Let's go."

Neirin loves the snow - he stomps his wellies in a soldier-like fashion, his arms swinging at his sides. "Can we go to the stream, please; I want to see the badgers?"

"Ok, but carefully - you know the rules, you wait for me before you go anywhere near the stream," Shenna reminds him, though she knows Neirin is sensible and she's taught him how to live safely in the forest.

Suddenly he stops and points up to a nearby branch. "Look mummy, it's Cyril," he laughs up at the red squirrel that seems to be watching the boy with interest. "We haven't seen him for ages."

Watching her son, Shenna enjoys his thrill of animals, always concerned if he hasn't seen one of his 'friends' for a while.

"It's been really cold over the last couple of weeks," she reminds Neirin, "Cyril probably just snuggled down for a while - but he looks fine."

The red squirrel turns its curious head to look at

Shenna as she approaches, and gives a flick of its bushy tail.

"Here," holding her hand out to Neirin, Shenna gives him a few peanuts from her pocket, "that boulder looks about right."

Neirin takes the peanuts and places them carefully on the flattest part of the large rock. Going back to his mum's side, he watches as the squirrel scoots down the tree and tucks in to the treat.

When the ground is clear of snow, Neirin often throws the peanuts on the ground just a couple of feet away and the squirrels actually don't mind him standing to watch as long as he is still and quiet.

Taking his mum's hand again, he looks up with a happy smile. "Did the badgers snuggle down, too?"

"Probably," Shenna tells him as they approach the stream, "but we'll see if we can see any tell-tale signs of activity."

They walk together in contented silence. The forest is full of birds and animals that an observant person can enjoy. Shenna takes out her binoculars and uses them to search the opposite river bank.

Handing them to Neirin, Shenna points about six feet up the rise of the bank. "There, do you see them…?"

Neirin points the binoculars in the direction his mum has indicated and sees the badgers' tracks. "They're alright," he looks up at Shenna with a grin, "I wonder if they'll have any cubs this year."

"Don't see why not...," she tells him, "...they haven't missed a year since we've lived here."

"How long have we lived here?" Neirin asks curiously.

"Your dad and I moved here about eight years ago - do you remember what I told you about your dad's work?" she asks Neirin.

"He looked after the forest," Neirin says proudly. "That's what I want to do."

"You do?" Shenna smiles down at her serious looking son and is thrilled to see the pride he has in a dad he never had the chance to meet. "Well, he would have loved sharing all of this with you. He used to enjoy teaching children all about the birds and animals that live in the forest and what we have to do to protect their homes."

"That's important," Neirin states as he takes hold of his mother's hand again, "or else they won't have anywhere to live and then they'll go ex...ex..."

"Extinct," Shenna finishes for him. "Yes, that's right and once that happens we never get to see them again."

"Ever?" Neirin looks up with startled eyes at his all-knowing mummy.

"Never again," she emphasises softly. "But we can all help to prevent that from happening - even in little ways that don't cost any money and very little time."

"We can?" he asks with a studious frown.

Nodding, Shenna points to a small clearing and a crisp packet that is sticking up out of the thin layer of snow. "Even if all we do is make sure that our rubbish is properly put in the bin."

Walking with him, Shenna allows Neirin to pick up the crisp packet with a gloved hand and shoves it into her pocket.

"We'd better get back," she tells him, "it's time to make tracks for your swimming lesson."

He doesn't complain, though Shenna can see that Neirin would have loved to stay a little longer in the forest. But then, he would always want more time - he loves the forest and the animals that live their. A real chip of the old block - he's just like you, Cade.

When they pull up in the leisure centre car park, Neirin spots his friend Tommy and waves excitedly out of the window. Tommy and his mum make their way over to the car just as Shenna unbuckles Neirin and they walk in to the centre together.

"I wasn't sure if anyone would turn up with all the snow," Gail comments as she helps Tommy into his swimming trunks.

"If you've lived here any length of time you don't let the weather dictate your life," Shenna smiles over to her friend. "Having said that," Shenna turns to survey the changing room in case she's missed seeing the other mum they usually meet up with, "I don't see Juliette and the twins - I didn't notice their car in the car park either."

No sooner had she got the words out than the woman herself, a rucksack on her back and a child clinging to each hand, rushes in to the changing room.

"Hi guys," Juliette sits both her boys down, does a quick flip of the rucksack off her back and unpacks two swimming kits. "Took me a while to get the car off the drive, but we're here - right kids!"

With the brisk efficient movements of a woman used to carrying out double the tasks in half the time, Juliette gets both boys into their swim trunks and piles everything else in a locker.

"You never cease to amaze me," Shenna laughs, and all three women and four boys make their way through to the pool.

Handing the children off to their instructors, the women get a hot drink and sit at their usual table at the side of the pool.

"I see Jason has another shiner," Shenna smiles over at the boy just getting into the pool with his brother.

"It's his own fault," Juliette shakes her head in despair, "he teases Jacob until he lashes out, only now they're getting older when the punches land they bruise."

"Does Jason ever clock him one back?" Gail asks taking a sip of her tea.

"That's the funny thing," Juliette tells them, "he really doesn't. It's like he knows he deserves it; that he's gone too far."

"Tommy's full of beans, as usual," Gail smiles fondly as her son gives a squeal before jumping off the side of the pool and into the water where a second instructor is waiting to ensure his safety.

Shenna watches Neirin, he's quieter than the others, standing back to observe. When it's his turn to jump in, however, he doesn't hesitate and surfaces quickly doing a brisk doggy-paddle to the side of the pool.

"Hey, Shenna," Gail calls her attention away from Neirin's efforts, "I heard some interesting news in the library the other day - it concerns your woods," she says with a cautionary lift of her brows.

"What was it about?" Shenna tears herself away from watching her son and gives her attention to Gail.

"It was kind of sketchy, but it sounds like someone is interested in that clearing just a little way from your cottage."

Shenna is shocked. "No one can build there - it isn't allowed."

"No...," Gail shakes her head after polishing off her tea; "...I suppose it's the opposite of that - someone reckons it could turn into an archaeological dig."

Frowning, Shenna considers the idea.

"Would that be so bad?" Juliette eyes Shenna's worried frown.

"That depends - can you find out any more about this?" she turns to Gail. "I'm not a forester like Cade, but I wouldn't feel right if I just let them dig the place up without making sure the animals and the forest itself didn't suffer in the process."

After the swimming lesson, Neirin goes for a play-date with the twins. When Shenna gets home the first thing she does is fire up her computer and starts a search for information.

Sure enough, when she looks on the Forestry Commission's web site, she finds reference to a possible archaeological dig taking place in The Iceni Forest.

Apparently there have been a number of artefacts found in the area pertaining to the Roman Britton era. The Iceni Forest was named after an Iron-age tribe known to have settled in this area, but apparently a Roman Britton settlement had followed after.

Switching her computer off, Shenna shrugs on a thick coat and boots then takes a walk out to the clearing.

It doesn't take long, the clearing is only about fifty yards from her front door, but the ground is treacherous underfoot and Shenna treads carefully.

What do you think of this then, Cade - an archaeological dig site in our forest? Sitting on a nearby tree stump, she looks up at a clear blue sky and smiles. I suppose it could be exciting, and Neirin would have some new learning opportunities.

She was just about to get to her feet when a tall, thick set man steps out of the trees and into the clearing on the opposite side.

He looks as surprised to see her as she is to see

him and they both stare unmoving.

Startled, a small flock of birds in a nearby tree take off in a noisy flap of wings, and the spell is broken.

She watches the man stride towards her and gets to her feet. "Can I help you?" she asks warily.

For a moment he doesn't speak, just stares down at her with a hard glint in his blue eyes.

"Are you Mrs Williams - owner of that cottage?" he asks pointing through the trees to the cottage where she lives.

He doesn't frighten Shenna, she's made of sterner stuff, but she is concerned as to why he is skulking about the forest.

"Who's asking?" Her eyes are as steady as his and notice a small frown of annoyance cross his brow.

"My name is Ryan Tempest and I'll be setting up an archaeological dig site here as soon as the snow clears."

Will you now - we'll just see about that!

"Well, Mr Tempest, as I've only just learned of the proposed project I have very little to say on the matter," she tells him stiffly. "But I will be keeping a very close eye on anything that might cause harm to the forest or its inhabitants - good day."

Ryan Tempest watches her march away towards the cottage and keeps watching until he sees her let herself in.

So, you are Mrs Williams - good to put a face to the name!

CHAPTER TWO

Walking into the library, Shenna shrugs out of her quilted coat and helps Neirin out of his.

"Ok," she sighs with a smile for her son, "let's see if anyone else made it in for story-time."

Pulling one of the double doors open, Neirin slips through and walks very sensibly up to the librarian's desk.

"We've come for story-time, Mrs Brennan," he states quietly, seriously.

"You remember where to go?" she asks and smiles over his head in greeting to Shenna. He gives a rapid nod of his head and looks up at his mum with questioning eyes.

"Go on over," she tells him, "I just need to have a quick word with Mrs Brennan."

Watching him walk through the tables and then turn left to the story corner, Shenna turns back to Mrs Brennan and says just one word, "Archaeology."

"Hmm, thought you might be in," the librarian purses her lips then ducks to retrieve some paperwork from a shelf. "I kept this by in case you did - it's an outline of the proposal and a bit of background information on Ryan Tempest, he's the head man who'll run things."

"Sounds like a forgone conclusion," Shenna frowns down at the papers in her hand. "Isn't there going to be any community consultation?"

"They don't need it for the go-ahead - which they've already got," Mrs Brennan informs her. "But there is going to be a Q & A session with display stands to show what they want to achieve and how they intend to do it. I've put it all in there for you," and points to the papers in Shenna's hand.

Walking away when another patron needs Mrs Brennan's attention; Shenna sits at a table nearby the story corner.

Watching Neirin, she wonders about her son's serious manner. It isn't that he doesn't join in or have fun, but he isn't boisterous like the other kids.

I wish you were here, Cade. Perhaps he takes

after you - I'll never know will I. He has your eyes, he even has your lop-sided smile when he's being mischievous - which isn't often enough.

With an annoyed shake of her head at her own thoughts, Shenna continues to watch as Neirin smiles happily watching the other children growl and paw the air pretending to be a wild lion, but he doesn't do the actions himself.

Am I doing this mothering thing right, Cade? You would have been so great with him - he said he wants to look after the forest, just like his dad - and it wouldn't surprise me if that's just what he does, too.

"Mum...?" Neirin stands watching her with his head tilted to one side.

"Hey...," she smiles brightly and takes her son's hand, "I was off in a world of my own, then," and gives a brief laugh at her own silliness.

"That's alright, mum...," Neirin looks up at her with serious eyes, "...I do that too - usually when I'm thinking about dad."

Pulling his coat on, Shenna studies her son. "Do you do that often?"

"When I'm in the forest, I do," he tells her with a nod.

"And here...in town?"

"Not so much, I know dad's with me when I'm in the forest," he tells her. "He told me that now I'm grown up I need to look out for you - that's my job now."

Trying not to let her shock show, Shenna tucks his scarf in and pulls on his woolly hat. "Do you dream about daddy a lot? I know you must miss having him around."

Frowning, Neirin shakes his head. "But daddy is always around," he tells her seriously, obviously wondering why she's asking such a daft question. "We talk about the forest and he tells me stories at bedtime." Then he frowns, really creasing his forehead as if in deep thought. "He says he can't come every night because he has other things he needs to take care of," then he looks at his mother with bewildered brown eyes - Cade's eyes. "What do you think angels do in heaven - do they have jobs like everyone else?"

Shenna has never seen this side of her son before, hadn't realised he has such an overactive and vivid imagination.

"Maybe," she hedges, "I've never really thought about it."

When they reach home, Shenna asks Neirin to

read quietly in his room while she takes a home tutoring session over the Skype. "Hi Jaden," she greets her first pupil of the week, "did you manage to do the math work I set you?"

"Hello Ms Williams," the blonde seven year old greets her favourite home teacher, "I did it all except the last two problems - I got stuck with those," she grimaces.

"Did you attempt to do them, or just leave them blank," Shenna asks.

"Oh, I tried," the little girl insists earnestly, "but I knew I wasn't doing it right."

Shenna nods pleased that Jaden had at least attempted the problems. "Ok, Jaden, fax it over to me and I'll take a look." She waits for the fax machine to spew out the girl's math paper then gives it a good look over.

"This is good work, Jaden," and watches the little girl's face light up with a smile. "Long multiplication and long division can be tricky - you got all of the division correct and most of the multiplication too." It doesn't take Shenna long to figure out where the girl when wrong with the last two sums. "Do you have your paper in front of you?" she asks Jaden then waits while the little girl runs to retrieve it from their fax machine.

"Got it," Jaden waves the paper and retakes her seat.

"Ok, if you look at the last two sums you'll see that you only put one zero at the beginning of the first line of multiplication and again on the second line," Shenna explains, "do you remember the rules of long multiplication?"

Jaden looks at the sums and starts writing on her paper, forgetting to answer her teacher's question. "Is that right?"

Shenna looks at the screen and smiles, "that's right, Jaden, well done. Just remember to put one less zero than the amount of figures in the number you are multiplying by - then reduce the zeros by one on each proceeding line."

The lesson goes well and Shenna is pleased with Jaden's progress. She is a quick study and actually enjoys learning.

When she goes to his bedroom to find Neirin, Shenna hears him talking to someone - then suddenly he stops and calls for her to come in.

"How did you know I was outside your door?" she asks lightly with a big smile.

"Daddy told me - he said he should go as it was probably time for my lessons."

"O..k," she drags out the tiny word with a frown then decides the best way to handle this situation is the same as she would if he had an imaginary friend, just accept and act natural until he grows out of it. "Well, if daddy ever wants to stay he can - maybe he'd enjoy watching you do your lessons?"

But Neirin just shakes his head as he climbs down off his bed. "I already told you, mum," he says in his best grown up voice, "dad has lots of other things to take care of, he doesn't have time to stay for long." And he brushes past her as if nothing he's said is out of the ordinary or in any way odd.

What the hell! Maybe I should have a word with the doctor - this is more than just an imaginary friend type situation...I think. Crikey!

That evening when Neirin is in bed, Shenna reads up on imaginary friends and reasons why children invent them. But instead of being reassured she finds herself reading about children who see spirits - apparently their young minds are more open to 'the other world' and their imaginary friends are actually spirits that they can see and talk to.

Bloody hell! What now - if he really believes he can talk to his dad Neirin won't be dissuaded, he's as stubborn as Cade ever was!

A week later and thankfully all the snow has disappeared. Neirin is having a sleepover with the twins and in exchange Shenna has promised to pick up all the information about the dig for Juliette.

Going to the library she looks around at all the displays about the archaeological dig that is shortly going to begin not fifty yards from her own front door.

"Hey, Gail," Shenna waves over at her friend, "have you had a chance to brows?"

Nodding, the other woman smiles radiantly. "And I've had a chance to talk to Ryan Tempest in person." Spinning her head from left to right and craning her neck for a better view, Gail plops back on her heels with a huff. "I hope he hasn't gone - he's soooo handsome - his voice was enough to make my knees go weak but his eyes…"

A deep gravelly voice sounds from behind them. "Ladies, have you had a chance to look around?"

Shenna turns to see Ryan Tempest giving Gail a charming smile. "Is Terry with you Gail?" she asks pointedly, not taking her eyes off of Ryan Tempest.

Her friend gives a nervous laugh. "Well of course he is," Gail frowns curiously at Shenna then aims another gushing smile at Ryan Tempest, "Terry is just getting us some tea from the refreshment stand - which you very thoughtfully provided."

"It's a cold night, a hot cup of tea warms the cockles," he returns her smile then turns to Shenna. "May I get you a cup, Mrs Williams?"

Gail falters. "You've met?" she asks.

"Briefly," Ryan nods. "Now, about that tea, may I get you a cup?"

"No, thank you," she tells him curtly, though she would dearly love a cup of hot tea.

"Then I'll leave you to wander round," he tells her, his smile taking on a hard edge. "The question and answer session will start in half an hour," and giving a brief nod of his head he walks away into the crowd.

"You don't like him...?" Gail asks surprise in her voice.

No I don't like him...but I don't know why, damn it!

"I don't know him," Shenna hedges and moves away to look at the info-stands. "I remember reading about some of this - this one in particular." Pointing to a photo of a dig site in Africa she reads the blurb supplied to remind her of the details. "Yes...quite a haul and Tempest had been in charge of that dig too."

I bet all of the digs on display here were headed up by the big-I-am Tempest!

"Wow," Gail looks at Shenna's snarling lips and takes a step back in mock fear, "you should see your face - if looks could kill, and that photo were the man himself, I swear he would have just keeled over and died."

"Who just died…?" Terry finally arrives back at Gail's side with two cups of steaming tea.

Gail takes her tea and swats his arm. "No one died - we were just talking."

"Where's Tommy," Shenna asks looking around at the same time, "I thought you were bringing him with you?"

"We did," Gail looks at her husband with a questioning frown, "what did you do with him?"

"The dig people are doing a special talk, over in the corner there, aimed at the kids." Terry points over with his chin.

Shenna watches the children's reactions and is pleased with what she sees. "Smart - getting the kids on-board, and to be fair they're doing an excellent teaching session."

"High praise indeed," Ryan Tempest tells her having found out that she herself is a teacher, "perhaps you will lend the dig your support now that you've seen we're not about to destroy the forest and everything living in it?"

Turning to him more fully, Shenna's eyes are cold as ice. "You don't need my support - you've got these people eating out of your hand."

Looking deep into her green eyes, Ryan wonders what is behind her open hostility. "Need…no, you're right, we don't need it - the dig will go ahead no matter what, it's too important not too," he tells her bluntly. "But you live right on top of the dig site, if you give it your blessing how could anyone else object?"

So…maybe that's what you were doing in my forest the other day, trying to find me to sell me the idea and head off the worst of the protests, should there be any. Clever…and conniving!

"Clever, but you overestimate my influence in the community," she tells him with a lift of her chin. "I home tutor some of the children in these parts, but that's the extent of my 'influence'."

A waving hand near the makeshift stage gets Ryan's attention. "I hope you'll all be staying for the talk, I'd be interested to hear what you think after." He addresses them all, but it's clear that it is Shenna's opinion he is courting.

They all three nod their heads but Shenna determines to leave the minute the talk is over. She isn't normally a coward and frowns at the idea of running away from another encounter with Tempest.

I am not running away - it's just a good opportunity to get some marking done while Neirin is on a sleepover with the twins. So there!

An hour later Shenna settles down in the cottage with a large mug of strong tea and a pile of marking. It isn't late, but she is already in her pyjamas and feeling ready to relax over her work.

She enjoys teaching, she doesn't need the money to enable her to live well, Cade had seen to her financial security before he'd died, but it gave her a lot of pleasure.

Shenna thought of Tommy Edmunds, Gail and Terry's almost six year old son and one of Neirin's best friends. He had been struggling at school and Gail had sought her out after getting a good report from Jaden's mum about her home tutoring. That was how they'd met, and now she was one of Shenna's very small circle of friends.

Tommy has benefitted greatly from their one to one sessions over the Skype connection she regularly uses. His self-confidence has gone from non-existent to moderately confident, and it pleases her greatly - especially now that Gail has enrolled him in the home tutoring scheme that knowing Shenna has introduced her to.

A solid knock on her front door makes Shenna jump and slop her tea over one of the papers she is marking.

"Bloody hell!" Getting up quickly she begins shaking the paper to get rid of the tea and walks distractedly across the lounge to open the door.

Startled, Shenna looks up into the amused face of Ryan Tempest and feels her temper rise. "Look what you made me do," and thrusts the tea stained paper under his nose, "I was busy marking papers when you decided to try knocking my door down." Taking a breath and a moment to actually look at him properly, Shenna feels an uncomfortable knot tightening in her stomach. Damn it...you shouldn't be here...you shouldn't...

"My apologies for disturbing you," his amusement has vanished along with his smile. "I'll leave you to your work."

"What!" she half shouts the word at him. "The damage is done - what the hell do you want?" Shenna has never been so ungracious in her life and has no idea what possessed her.

His own temper flaring, Ryan watches her push her long mane of red hair back over her narrow shoulders then realises she is actually wearing her pyjamas.

"I really do apologies for disturbing you," he tells Shenna, his deep quiet voice rumbling up her spine. "I merely wanted some feedback - I looked for you, and your friends, after the talk but they told me you'd had to leave."

Feeling an idiot, standing at her front door in her pyjamas, not to mention freezing half to death, Shenna moves back and waves an arm to invite Tempest in.

"I'll just be a minute," she tells him and waves a hand towards an armchair to offer him a seat.

"If you're going to change, you needn't do so on my account," Ryan tells her and feels his lips tilt up at the corner.

Blushing, Shenna continues to her bedroom where she quickly pulls on a fleece lined tracksuit - one she would normally wear to go for a run in just this sort of weather.

"Tea...?" she asks when Ryan looks up on her return to the sitting-room. "Or I do have coffee...I just don't drink it as much." And I'm rambling. Just slow down and hope he says no to the tea then get him out of here…fast!

"I'd love one, thanks," and actually smiles so that his blue eyes twinkle at her.

Damn!

"How do you take it?"

"Black no sugar, thanks." Ryan watches her turn to enter the kitchen and finds himself focusing on her neat bottom. She's taken care of herself. Trim and toned despite having a child…a son…Neirin, an unusual name for a boy. Perhaps he's named for his dead father? No, no…his name was Cade…

"Here we go," Shenna breaks into his thoughts by handing him a mug of tea.

Young to be a widow…I wonder what happened.

Retaking her seat on the settee where her papers were now gathered up, Shenna tucks her legs up under her and watches him over her mug, only to find herself being studied in return.

"What do you want to ask me?" she asks when the silence lengthens uncomfortably and he still hasn't stopped studying her. "Surely you got enough feedback from the people who were still there."

Shaking his head, Ryan sits forward in his seat and a different expression, that she has a hard time defining, comes over his handsome features.

"Not as informed," he tells her, causing Shenna to sit up straighter, "they meant well, most of them, but it was mostly superficial hand shaking and polite smiles - you were mingling, you know most of these people; what were they really thinking? Did they voice any actionable concerns - anything that we can do something to allay?"

He actually sounds concerned - maybe I haven't given him enough credit.

"There were a few hardliners, you won't change their minds no matter what - they just don't like the idea of being invaded on mass by a bunch of strangers."

"Six," Ryan interrupts her, "that's how many of us there will be - no more than six."

"Ok," she nods thoughtfully, "I suppose I could let that snippet of information circulate when I next go in to the library."

He nods but stays silent.

"Mostly it was parents who use the forest with their children who had the greatest concerns," she informs him, and again gives that thought some consideration. "You halfway won them over with your teaching session that you already know I approved of." Again he nods but to her annoyance continues to remain silent and a frown darkens her brow. "I suppose you could build on that by setting aside a visitors area - perhaps something structured so that you don't get people dropping by at all times of the day," she suggests, and this time she determines to stay quiet and sips her tea.

Reading her perfectly, Ryan is pleased that his ploy of forcing her to speak has gleaned some useful information.

"By structured, do you mean a time-table for visitors or an actual structure to house a display in?"

"Both, if possible," she suggests and finds herself getting interested in the teaching possibilities. "If you could set something up one day a week I could organise a couple of teaching sessions grouping them by age - I already take groups into the forest, that would expand the children's interest nicely and tie in some local history into the bargain."

Ryan is fascinated by the glow of enthusiasm he can see growing and watches her mind tick over with a dozen different thoughts. Not the stern widow woman now are you. It's like you've just come alive after a long sleep…or maybe I'm just being stupidly fanciful. Get a grip, Tempest!

Getting to his feet Ryan looks down at Shenna, her feet drawn up under her on the settee. "If you wouldn't mind putting your idea down on paper - and anything else you might think of," he urges as he watches her uncurl herself like a contented cat, "I'd be very grateful and will give your idea of a visitors centre some serious thought."

He watches her move barefoot towards him, no doubt to show him out but he doesn't move.

You even walk like a cat, all grace and beauty with a mane of red hair any cat would enjoy having stroked…

"Mr Tempest…?" Shenna tilts her head to look up at him with questioning eyes.

Cats eyes…green and slightly tilted up at the corners…

"Mr Tempest…are you alright?" she asks her growing concern in her voice as well as her eyes.

Giving his head a shake, Ryan manages to break free of her spell. "Sorry…sorry…just getting carried away with the visitors centre idea." Moving to the door he allows Shenna to open it and steps out into the cold evening air. "Thank you again, Mrs Williams, you've been most helpful."

CHAPTER THREE

Having slept fitfully again, Shenna moves around the kitchen, getting breakfast for herself and Neirin, in less than her usually efficient manner.

"Is that daddy's shirt?" Neirin sits himself down at the breakfast table and watches his mother go from cupboard to fridge and back to the table.

Looking down at herself, Shenna realises she has forgotten that she got out of bed in the middle of the night again and pulled on one of Cade's shirts she still kept.

"Yes, I sometimes use them as a nightie," she explains, but gives herself a rap on the knuckles for not changing as she usually did before Neirin could see her in it.

Watching his mother pour his favourite cereal into a bowl, Neirin appears untroubled and quite content with her answer.

Am I feeling guilty because my carelessness could have upset my son, or because I felt the need to wear one of Cade's shirts in the first place? The latter - I think. But it worked…again…I didn't have any more inappropriate dreams about Ryan Tempest!

And where are they coming from anyway - I don't even like the man! Why would I even dream about letting him put his hands all over me that way!

"Mum?" Neirin had clearly been trying to get her attention for a while as his voice was full of annoyance.

"Yes…yes…just thinking about jobs I need to do - sorry, Neirin."

"Are we going to the library today - June is coming in to read the story and she's really funny?" His smile lights up his face and give his brown eyes, Cade's eyes, a warm glow.

"Are you sure, Neirin - I thought June was on holiday?"

"That was last week, mum," her young son informs her patiently.

"Really…?" Shenna frowns contemplating the

disappearance of so much time. Has it really been two weeks since Ryan Tempest darkened my door? "No problem, we'll go for a walk first and then go to the library - we'll be a bit early for story-time but we can read together for a while." Her smile is warm and loving; Shenna likes nothing more than spending time with her son. Neirin is so grown up for his age; an unusually serious young man, he just loves to learn.

"Ok," he readily agrees and concentrates on finishing his cereal and milk.

When they step out of the cottage a short time later, Shenna is glad she told Neirin to put his woolly hat and scarf on.

"It's not as warm as it looks," she turns to her son watching him pull on his gloves, "the sun is cold, yet."

"Hmm," Neirin murmurs as he takes his mum's hand, "but it won't snow again."

Frowning, Shenna contemplates her son's firm conviction. "What makes you say that - did Cyril whisper in your ear when you last gave him some peanuts."

Giving a low giggle, Neirin looks up at his mum and gives a shake of his head. "Squirrels can't talk, you know that," he tells her and swings both their hands up and back in the air playfully.

"So, how do you know it won't snow again this year?"

Shenna finds herself holding her breath waiting for his answer.

"Daddy told me," Neirin smiles up at his mum. "He said I would be able to play out more now that the snow has disappeared and wouldn't be back again."

Oh, heck! I knew it. Just let it go, Shenna - just distract him and get his thoughts channelled elsewhere! If you can't do that you have no business calling yourself a teacher!

"Well, let's make the most of this weather and head through here," and indicated a narrow trail that the inexperienced walker might miss.

The ground was a mulch of thawed out soil and decaying leaves but there were visible fresh animal tracks ahead of them.

"What do you think made those?" she asks Neirin, who promptly crouches down to get a better look.

"I'm not sure," he tips his head up to look at her, "something bigger than Cyril but not as big as a deer."

"That's very good," she beams a smile of approval and takes his hand when he stands up again. "Can you think of any of your other animal friends that might fit into that category?"

Neirin shakes his head and frowns. "Only the badgers, but they don't live on this side of the river."

"Actually, I think you might be right," she crouches down next to the next lot of clear paw prints. "I think there might be a new badger's set somewhere around here - new neighbour for the river bank badgers."

Neirin looks up at his mum wide-eyed. "Can we look for them, mummy - can we see if we can find their home?"

But Shenna shakes her head with a sad smile. "We'll definitely come back another day and see if we can follow the trail to their home - but if we don't make our way back soon we'll miss story time with June."

His little face looks torn. On the one hand he loves to hear June read stories at the Library - she makes them all laugh and sometimes makes them jump at the scary bits - but this could be a whole new family of badgers that have moved in on their side of the river.

"The badgers will still be here this afternoon," she tells him when he only stands looking in the direction the little footprints lead. "If you work hard on your sums and your drawing I'll bring you back for an hour then. Ok?"

His huge smile is all the encouragement Shenna needs as Neirin retakes her hand and almost pulls her back along the track in a hurry now to get to the library.

As they near the cottage they both turn at the sound of raised voices coming from the clearing.

A woman is shouting the odds at a group of younger people carrying various packages from a modest four-by-four to a port-a-cabin. However, when she spies Shenna and Neirin watching, her manner abruptly changes.

Shenna takes Neirin to the car and straps him in to his seat. When she turns the woman from the clearing has made her way over and is almost to the car.

"I'm so sorry if we disturbed you," the woman holds out a hand to Shenna and gives a smile that doesn't reach her cold blue eyes, "I'm Felicity, I'm helping to head up this dig and we're just getting supplies and other essentials transported in." With a flick of her head towards the dig site, Felicity barely hides a snarl. "We seem to have been landed with a raw crew - they have no idea about archaeology and are probably hoping for an exciting adventure to talk about over a drink back home - but they've got another think coming."

Poor kids! Maybe they are looking for a bit of excitement along the way but where's the harm in that!

"They sound young, full of beans," Shenna gives a placatory smile, "but youngsters willing to work for no pay are usually eager to learn, or why would they do it?"

Felicity doesn't answer, just giving a dismissive grunt instead. "I'll tell them to keep the noise down," she snaps and strides away

They get to the Library in plenty of time and read quietly together while they wait for the story corner to set up.

"Hey, good to see you," Gail grins enthusiastically. Tommy sits by Neirin and they look at books together.

"How's the home tutoring going," Shenna asks looking at Tommy then back to Gail. "He certainly looks happier."

"Oh, he is," Gail smiles dotingly at her son, "it seems to suit him much better. We still have lots of contact with other children and the schedule we've worked out lets us do lots of other activities - like this," and she waves a hand over to the story corner and the growing number of children gathering there with their parents. "And he loves the rambles in the forest you do with them - I don't think he even thinks of it as learning, he just has fun and doesn't realise how much knowledge he's taking in at the same time."

"Then I'm doing my job right," Shenna smiles, pleased to hear that her teaching in the forest is going over well, "children learn far more if they're having fun while doing it."

I really do have a great life…thanks to your thoughtfulness, Cade.

"Hi." Juliette ushers her sons over to the other children sitting cross-legged on the floor then comes back to sit with Gail and Shenna. "How's the dig going," she asks Shenna and raises her eyebrows when Shenna frowns.

"Mostly I hardly know they're there," she tells them.

"But…," Juliette persists.

"Well, Neirin and I were out in the woods when we heard a lot of shouting and couldn't help but watch to see what all the ruckus was about." Her frown deepens with remembering. "I got Neirin strapped into his car-seat and had just closed the door when I realised a woman from the dig had come over. She's a piece of work," Shenna recalls the lovely looking woman's face twisting into an ugly sneer. "She made out like she was apologising for the youngsters being so noisy - youngsters she can't stand…by the way - yet she was the one we had heard doing the yelling." Shenna looks at the other two women, "I really don't think I'm going to like having her for a neighbour - let's hope this dig doesn't take long."

"Is her name Felicity Mayfield?" Gail asks her eyes narrowing with curiosity.

"She just introduced herself as Felicity, so I think there's a good chance it is - why?"

"Well, she's almost as big as Ryan Tempest in archaeology circles," Gail informs them, "which begs the question, why is she even here?"

"You seem remarkably well informed," Juliette laughs at Gail's gossipy inflection, "why do you think she's here?"

"Ah, well, rumour has it that she has the hots for Mr Tempest - they have done other digs together but more-so in the last couple of years." Gail sits back with a self-congratulatory smile.

"Hmm, well that could be a good thing," Shenna muses then continues when she sees both her friends confused faces. "It'll keep him out of my hair." If not my dreams…but you don't need to know about that!

The dig site is virtually set to start actual digging. Ryan Tempest has had a smaller port-a-cabin delivered at his own expense to act as a visitors centre. The more he'd thought about the idea the more he thought it was a good one and deserved to be done properly.

"Sadie, Roz," he calls out to a couple of the students, "have you got the box with the display artefacts in?" When they confirm that they have he asks them to take it into the allotted visitors centre. "Just set them out however you think best - label each piece so that visitors will know what they're looking at then tell me when you've finished."

The two girls give a smiling nod and a wave then go off to do his bidding.

There are two larger port-a-cabins, both set into the trees at odd angles to fit in without damaging the surroundings. One is used for female sleeping quarters and as a basic lab for cleaning and cataloguing any finds. The second acts as male sleeping quarters and as the main office. Both have basic wash facilities and lighting powered by a generator. They even have separate port-a-loos for males and females next to them.

When Ryan enters the office he finds Felicity going through some of the paperwork checking off site inventory for tools and supplies.

"Anything not arrived?" he asks when the leggy blonde looks up at him with a frown.

"We're still waiting on some of the tools, but nothing we can't make a start without," she tells him then stands and places a hand on his arm, enjoying the feel of his innate strength. "You've been gone a long time, any problems on the money end?"

"Not now," Ryan turns to look at the woman who has been his lover on and off over the last five or six years and actually feels himself cringe away from her touch, "I had to do the dance with our backers, laying out the basic costs and benefits to them as named benefactors."

Sliding her hand up and down his arm, Felicity moves closer. "Poor you, it can be tedious pandering to the money men but we couldn't do what we do without them."

Not wanting to give her any invitation, Ryan moves away from her touch ostensibly to pick up more paperwork. "I'm surprised the visitors centre wasn't set up while I was away - you've had at least a week," he tells her and watches the temper light her eyes.

"Why on earth you're indulging that woman's idea is beyond me," she throws her hands up in the air, "haven't we got enough to do without a damned visitors centre?"

Looking at Felicity, Ryan realises why he's pulled back from her lately. She's grown ugly over the last couple of years - not in looks, she takes care of herself well even when she gets her hands dirty working on site, but her attitude towards others is bitchy and condescending.

"I happen to think it's a good idea," he tells her firmly, leaving no room for argument. "The local population is fairly young and has shown an active interest in the forest prior to our arrival - it's good practice to get the local community involved."

"Well, on your head be it," she tells him and stomps out of the office to start yelling at anyone on hand.

Maybe this should be our last dig…working together isn't as enjoyable as it once was and the sex just isn't as appealing.

Ryan had once cared for Felicity, had thought their futures might join at some point, but her growing meanness and unpleasant treatment of the students they worked with and relied on had pushed those thoughts aside.

He's tried to separate himself from her as gently as possible, not wanting to hurt her feelings, sure that she genuinely cares for him. But it doesn't seem to be working - he might have to be more direct for her to take him seriously. Not something to look forward to!

Going over to the visitors centre, Ryan takes a look at what the students have done so far.

"This is great," he smiles and nods while looking at the neat hand-written cards set at the back of each artefact, "you girls have got a knack for the succinct - just enough info to tell them what's what without confusing the hell out of them."

Sadie and Roz both glow with pride. "We thought we'd draw a map of the immediate area showing where each piece was found," Sadie looks up hopefully at Ryan.

"Good idea, is that why you put the local pieces separate?"

"Yes," Roz speaks up now that she knows he isn't going to bite their heads off like Felicity usually does, "we thought we'd gradually build up another map showing what we find from the dig - it could show any living areas we might come across or just the artefacts and what they would have been used for..." Roz tails off as Felicity enters the room.

"That's thinking some way ahead, but I like your optimism and ideas," he tells them. "Keep thinking up ways to improve the centre and run anything you come up with by me, ok?"

He hears Felicity give a snort of disgust behind him and turns to guide her out.

"What's wrong, Felicity, the kids are doing a great job - let's not squash their enthusiasm," he tells her not hiding his annoyance.

At that, Felicity reigns herself in and pulls on an indulgent smile. "You always do get on better with the youngsters than I," she gushes and again touches his arm with an intimate caress, "it just galls me that we have to rely on them instead of hiring a more experienced crew. It all comes down to the damned money-men - they expect us to perform miracles on a pittance!"

Ryan is no longer fooled by her pretence of affability; he has seen a side of Felicity that he can't un-see no matter how she tries to hide it.

"Just try not to run them off in the first couple of weeks," he tells her, then feels bad for the look of hurt that crosses her face. "I just meant, try to think of them as future archaeologist that need a bit of seasoning and encouragement - there aren't enough of us out in the wide world," he smiles trying to lighten the mood.

"The fact that the last lot of students couldn't hack the work wasn't my fault," Felicities spine straightens and Ryan gets ready for another of her tirades.

Back in the visitors centre the two girls watch and feel sorry for Ryan.

"I don't know why he puts up with her," Roz tells Sadie. "It's not like he needs her - there are plenty of other archaeologists who would give their eye teeth to work with him."

Sadie nods in agreement. "We were lucky to get chosen for this - putting up with her majesty is a small price to pay for working with the best," and her young eyes become moony as she looks at her hero trying to fend off the she-bitch from hell.

"That's enough, Felicity," Ryan finally snaps when

she starts calling the students lazy good-for-nothings, "if you can't work alongside them perhaps you should think about leaving before they do!"

Shocked to the core Felicity rounds on him, "You would chose them over me?" Her eyes go wide when she sees the answer clearly in his, then decides that tears might work better on him as they have in the past. Her bottom lip trembles and her eyes obligingly fill with tears. "I can't believe you would treat me this way after all we've been to each other," she tells him and walks off to the women's living quarters to make a dramatic exit and cut off any chance of him asking her to leave.

I don't believe it! You can't treat me like an old rag you've finished wiping your hands on. I won't let you, damn it!

Troubled by her tears, Ryan isn't even sure they were real. Running a hand back through his short blond hair he tries to calm his temper.

Christ! She really has a way of getting under my skin lately. I don't know why the hell I let her talk me into letting her come - she hasn't shown any enthusiasm for the dig at all, and the way she treats the rest of the team I'll be lucky if they see the job out!

Sitting at his desk, Ryan pulls some paperwork in

front of him and decides to get the tedious task out of the way. Paperwork is the bane of his life, he prefers being outdoors getting his hands dirty.

A couple of hours later Sadie and Roz give him an excuse to ditch the paperwork that he hasn't quite managed to finish.

"Just thought we'd let you know we think we've finished in the visitors centre," Sadie puts her head round the door and looks pleased with herself, "unless there's anything else you want adding or changing."

Getting up from the desk, Ryan stretches his broad chest and causes both girls to give inward sighs of admiration.

"Ok, let's take a look," he smiles encouragingly and follows them over to the smaller port-a-cabin.

On entering he tries to imagine how a visitor that knows nothing about archaeology might view the display. The first thing he sees on the opposite wall as he walks in the door is a poster telling the visitor about the Iron Age and the tribe the forest is named after. Then it details the Roman Britain era giving dates and a bit about the way life is generally thought to have been lived in those times.

Ryan nods and smiles, impressed by the local

information the girls have put together. "This is good, it'll get the local interest going right from the start."

Then he moves to the artefact displays – he saw the local recent finds display earlier but now it is complete and fully labelled up.

"Again, you've really emphasised the local interest by keeping these items together and the info' cards are great."

Both girls are beaming, really appreciating his comments.

Then he moves to a display showing a few general Iron Age and Roman Britain artefacts that he was able to procure to enhance the centre.

On the walls he sees the maps the girls had told him about earlier. One showing where each of the local pieces had been found and the other left blank but a heading over it saying 'Artefacts found during this dig'.

"Very impressive," he looks from Sadie to Roz and gives a nod of approval. "Don't change a thing, you've done an exceptional job."

"Thanks," Roz smiles shyly, "we had fun with it and it'll be great to add each piece we find to the map and the display shelf. We just put those books there to fill the space for now and to give the visitors something to read if they wanted more information on something."

Again Ryan nods and looks at the archaeology text books that the girls had obviously taken from their own belongings.

"How would you feel about helping to run the centre one day a week," he asks and enjoys the enthusiastic nods they give in reply. "Ok, well you can do the first day together to get a feel for it," and to get your confidence in talking to the public he thinks to himself, "then you can probably take it in turns – one in here one working on the dig – does that sound ok?"

"Sounds great," Sadie's smile goes from ear to ear as she looks from Ryan to Roz who is also smiling fit to burst.

"Good, lock up here and we'll start getting our hands dirty outside – it's time to start finding something to put on your recent finds display."

The work is tedious and backbreaking – but all of the workers enjoy it. Roz and Sadie continue to chatter about different ideas for the visitors centre while they work – Paul and Carl, two archaeology students in their final year of study, work silently side by side and Ryan helps with the digging while keeping an eye on what everyone else is doing and giving the odd piece of advice where needed.

The only person not present on the dig site is Felicity who is conspicuous by her absence. Not that anyone comments on it, certainly Sadie and Roz are relieved that the older woman isn't around, though they didn't think she would shout and rave at them while Ryan was present.

When they stop for the day, Ryan assesses their progress and thanks them all for their efforts. It isn't easy work as the ground is still hard, even frozen in parts, but no one has complained.

"Let's have a good meal and a drink," he suggests to the delight of the crew, "then you can do as you like – either stay on site or go into the town but I would ask you not to get drunk or upset the locals. We're going to be here a while and we don't want to get off on the wrong foot."

When Felicity does finally emerge, she is quiet and helps to dish up the meal that Roz and Paul have prepared.

Ryan begins to think he's misjudged her and tries to bring her into the conversation.

"We managed to clear a good bit of ground

today," he tells Felicity, "I think it might get a bit easier from tomorrow, the weather forecast says milder temperatures can be expected for at least the next week."

Nodding her head but keeping it bent over her plate, Felicity just says, "That's good," then continues to eat her meal in silence.

Bloody hell, I must really have hurt her feelings – I thought she was tougher than that. Damn!

"Do you fancy a drink in town," Paul asks Roz when they begin clearing the dishes.

Roz blushes and nods her head while nervously biting down on her bottom lip.

Sadie decides to stay in and do some necessary clothes washing and Carl gets out the textbooks he's brought with him to get a few hours quiet study in.

Ryan would ordinarily have asked Felicity to join him for a drink in the office, but he doesn't want to encourage her flirtations or give her the wrong idea. Their physical relationship has been over for months and that's the way he wants to keep it, so he takes himself off to finally finish the unavoidable paperwork.

CHAPTER FOUR

Pacing his office after breakfast with the crew next morning, Ryan Tempest is not best pleased. Felicity had cornered him, but instead of flirting, she had been subdued and apologetic.

Apparently, her back was up about the visitors' centre because Mrs Williams had been complaining unnecessarily about the noise of the dig and had been quite unpleasant to her when she had tried to apologies.

And I thought she was open to the dig taking place – just shows how wrong you can be! Well, I'll warn her to keep well away from it if that's going to be her attitude!

Not checking the time, Ryan makes his way the

short distance to the cottage. He gives the door a firm knock and waits for Mrs Williams to answer.

Dressed in one of Cade's shirts and just the underwear she wore beneath it, Shenna answers the door in a sleepy stupor as it is still only six-thirty in the morning and she'd had a late night lesson planning.

"Yes," she frowns up at Ryan and blinks, bemused, "is…is something wrong?"

He looks at her sleep-tousled hair spilling over her shoulders and the shirt she is wearing, which is obviously a man's, and thinks he has never seen anything so adorable – which only serves to annoy him further.

"I understand you had words with Felicity, my site coordinator yesterday?" His voice comes over as bitingly accusatory.

Raising her eyebrows in confusion, Shenna blinks her large green eyes and stares for a moment. "You got me up to talk about your site coordinator – she apologised for the noise, end of story."

Looking at his watch for the first time, Ryan realises his mistake but decides what's done is done. "You were apparently quite abusive to her and I won't tolerate it. We've done everything possible to accommodate the local community – a couple of the students spent most of the day yesterday setting up the visitors' centre you suggested, opening times will be posted as soon as practicably possible." He takes a breath and frowns as his insides tighten. Why are you looking at me so confused and…bloody hell! "You're welcome to use the visitors centre as we discussed but steer clear of my staff!"

With that, Ryan turns and strides off through the trees and back to his office in the clearing.

Shenna watches his retreating back until he is out of site. At first, she is just stunned, but then she grows angry.

What the hell was that all about? Did he say I'd been abusive – to who and when? What the flaming heck is that lunatic on about!

Even a usually relaxing shower doesn't calm her down. Now that Shenna is clear-headed, she is as mad as Ryan Tempest had been.

How dare you come to my door and start shouting the odds. I'll give you 'steer clear of my staff' you arrogant trumped up hole digger!

Pulling on jeans and a jumper, she checks on Neirin and finds him still fast asleep.

Locking the front door quietly behind her, Shenna

marches up to Ryan's office and steps up and through the doorway. She stands hands on hips her long red hair still hanging in damp tendrils down her back.

When he turns to look at her Ryan is dumbstruck.

"Don't you dare come to my home shouting the odds – I have no intention of coming anywhere near any of your staff and you can stick your visitors' centre where the sun doesn't shine!"

Turning on her heels, Shenna doesn't wait for his reply but marches off back to her cottage and locks the door behind her.

Leaning back against it she tries to work out what just happened. The last time she'd spoken to Ryan Tempest he had seemed reasonable and enthusiastic for her input, now he was telling her to keep away – why?

Her day continues as it started – one thing after another either went wrong, wasn't where it should be, couldn't be found, or just refused to work.

On the telephone to a repair man, Shenna gives a huge sigh of capitulation, "Ok, ok, if you can't come today or tomorrow it will have to be Thursday," and waits while her appointment is booked in and she is given a job reference number. "Thank you," she tells him as she scribbles the information on a pad.

Now what – how am I supposed to give lessons without my internet and Skype connection? Damn!

"Mum...?" Neirin looks cautiously at his mother having heard her annoyed voice on the telephone.

Shenna looks round and walks over to smooth a hand over his worried brow.

"Not to worry, Neirin," she reassures her son, "I'll phone around to let everyone know that lessons are off – probably for the whole week – and then we can go out walking if you'd like?"

Nodding enthusiastically, Neirin gives his mum a lovely smile.

"Can we go right to the top of the big hill?" he asks excitedly. "I really like looking down from there...and it is sunny today," he encourages, and his smile turns into a bright grin when Shenna nods her agreement.

"Let's take a packed lunch – by the time we reach the top it'll be just about lunch time." Shenna goes to walk towards the kitchen but stops and turns back to Neirin. "You're the most precious part of my life," she tells him with a gentle hand lain against his cheek, "and you have all the very best parts of your father in you. Like that cheeky grin," she laughs and playfully ruffles his hair.

"Will you tell me about daddy again," he smiles up at her, "when we get to the top of the hill – will you tell me some new stories?"

"It will be my pleasure...now you go and read for a bit while I prepare our packed lunch." This time Shenna does head for the kitchen and just in time to spare Neirin the worry of seeing his mummy cry.

She cut the cheese and made sandwiches with buttered whole-wheat bread, put some salad in a lidded bowl and got an apple and an orange each out of the fruit bowl.

"Ok, are we ready?" Shenna calls out while packing a drink in her backpack along with all the food she's prepared.

"I'm ready, mum," Neirin calls out from his bedroom, then appears at the top of the stairs and carefully makes his way down. "Is this ok?" he asks looking down at his padded gilet and long sleeved lightweight jumper beneath.

Crouching down to look into his serious young face, Shenna gives him a motherly hug.

"Muuuum," he complains as she continues to hug him, but when she pulls away, he is smiling happily.

"Us mums need hugs too," Shenna tells him as she stands and pulls on her backpack. Opening the front door, Shenna steps out to feel a mild chill in the air. "It's not too bad, what you've got on should be just right."

Their climb is long; mainly because they both enjoy looking at animal tracks and various birds they spot either sitting in trees or pecking at the ground for bugs and worms.

By the time they reach the summit it is indeed lunch time, as Shenna predicted.

"Shall we go to our log?" she asks Neirin when he joins her.

Nodding enthusiastically he runs ahead with the energy of youth that Shenna can only envy.

Unpacking their lunch and setting it between them on the fallen tree trunk, Shenna is struck by the familiarity of the situation. She's done this many times with Neirin, of course, but right now it's Cade that comes to mind.

"Your dad and I loved this spot so much," she tells Neirin and watches his upturned face brighten with interest. "This was the first place your dad brought me when he was offered the job of forester. It didn't take much persuading to get me to move out here after I saw that," and she waves a hand at the view of the valley below them and the countryside visible for miles around.

"I never want to leave here," Neirin tells her seriously, his young face so adult looking. "When I grow up I'm going to be a forester right here, just like dad."

Not quite five, Shenna never ceases to be amazed by his maturity. Sometimes his knowledge and understanding makes her very proud, at others it makes her wonder if living in the isolation of the forest is the best thing for Neirin.

He has lots of play-dates and interaction with other children; she's made sure of that. But his seriousness and un-childlike observations often give her pause.

"Don't you think you might like to live in a house like Tommy's or the twins'?" she asks with a questioning frown over worried eyes.

His shocked expression tells her better than any words that she couldn't be more wrong.

"Never!" he states uncompromisingly. "I love our house and the forest, and I love being close to dad." It's Neirin's turn to wear a worried frown, "Are we leaving?" he asks quietly, as if not wanting to speak the thought out loud and make it real.

Considering her son's distressed face for just a moment, Shenna reassures him. "Not for as long as you're happy here – but I am asking you to tell me if that ever changes," she tells him with a smile to lighten the mood. "If you ever find it too lonely you'll tell me, right?"

Nodding with a huge grin of relief, Neirin turns his little face to regard the beautiful panorama before him and knows he will never leave.

An hour later, when they are packing away all of their lunch things and checking they haven't left any litter on the ground, Shenna laughs in the middle of telling Neirin a story about his father.

"He was so funny," her laughter is full of love and fond remembering, "I couldn't stop laughing when he skidded and literally fell at my feet – the open yogurt he was carrying slopped all over him."

Neirin squeals with boyish laughter that Shenna is thrilled to hear.

"We were so happy," she tells him and lays a hand to his cheek. "We didn't have as long together as we would have liked, but the time we had was precious and filled with love." Her thumb is caressing his cheek so gently, her soft green eyes filling with emotion, "When I told daddy about you he was so happy, so proud to think that a part of him would live on in you."

They walked back to the cottage in a more contemplative but companionable silence.

"What the heck does he want now?!" Shenna strides up to the cottage with Neirin in tow and scowls at Ryan Tempest.

"Mrs Williams," Ryan gives her a nod in greeting then turns his attention to Neirin. Holding a hand out to him, Ryan introduces himself, "I'm Ryan Tempest, one of the archaeologists working in the clearing."

Neirin doesn't take Ryan's hand but emulates his mother's scowl.

"You made my mum cross," he states with all the simplicity of a child's logic.

Ryan nods, drops his hand and turns his attention back to Shenna. "Quite the little man," he acknowledges with a half-smile.

"Neirin will be five next week, though his comprehension and vocabulary far exceed his age," she tells him with no little pride and a lot of annoyance. "What do you want, Mr Tempest?"

His own annoyance starts to rise and his steel blue eyes cloud over. "I merely wanted to make peace – we are going to be living and working in close proximity for a while – wouldn't it be better for all concerned to do so amicably?"

Her eyes fly wide in shock. "It was you who came to my door at an ungodly time of the morning accusing me of abusing your staff – though where the heck you got that idea from I can't imagine," Shenna huffs loudly and makes to walk past him to her front door.

However, one small side step and Ryan has her effectively blocked.

"Get out of my way, you arrogant man," she scolds quietly for her son's sake.

"I also came to apologise for the early hour of my visit," he continues as if she hasn't spoken, "and to offer to show both of you around the site."

He hadn't at all, but the thought struck him now as a good one.

"You...you want to show us round...?" Shenna is still scowling only now it is in disbelief. "You told me to stay away from your staff – how am I supposed to do that if I'm walking round the site?"

She knows she is being difficult but decides he deserves to be given a hard time after the wakeup call he gave her that morning.

Pursing his lips then forcibly relaxing his expression, Ryan moves aside. "You don't forgive easily," he tells her then looks at Neirin, "but I would have thought, being a teacher, you might put your son's needs before your own."

When he looks back at her, Shenna can see that all the annoyance and arrogance has gone out of him.

"Ordinarily I would jump at the chance to give Neirin any new learning experience," and her chin lifts defiantly. "However, I..."

"That's great then," he cuts her off abruptly. "You look like you've had a tiring day so perhaps now is not the best time," he tells her and causes Shenna's spine to straighten reflexively. "Would tomorrow suit?"

Noticing that Neirin is looking up at her expectantly, Shenna nods and smiles down at her son, "Would you like that?"

"I think so," he tells her cautiously, and she realises that he is being mindful of her feelings.

Brightening her smile to show him that all is well, Shenna turns her attention back to Ryan Tempest. "That sounds like a yes to me," Shenna agrees. "What time would you want us?"

Ryan has to drag his thoughts out of the gutter, for some reason he finds himself having to do that every time he looks at this woman.

"How would mid-morning suit?"

"About tenish?" Shenna suggests and smiles stiffly at his nod of agreement. "We'll see you tomorrow then, Mr Tempest."

Ryan watches as she moves past him and enters the cottage. The boy is older than his years – he narrows his eyes still seeing the boy's eager anticipation of learning about something new.

Is it a natural instinct or one that his mother has instilled in him?

The following day Ryan sees for himself how eager Neirin is to learn and how readily he absorbs information. After showing both Shenna and Neirin around the site, pointing out the plans for the dig and the visitors centre, he introduces Neirin to Sadie, one of his volunteer students.

"Would you mind a little helper for a while," Ryan asks the young woman. "I want to show Mrs Williams the visitors centre you and Roz worked so hard on."

"Sure thing," Sadie smiles brightly at Neirin and waves him over, "come and have a go."

Ryan watches as Sadie shows the boy a roll of tools that she is using to carefully remove the soil to find anything that might be hidden beneath it. When he is happy that they are both getting along, Ryan turns to Shenna and says, "Shall we," and waves a hand to indicate the smaller port-a-cabin.

As soon as she walks in the door Shenna is impressed. She reads the posters and the maps the girls have put up then inspects the showcases that hold the shards of pottery and other items found in the area. Then Shenna moves over to a display of items from other dig sites with explanations of what the items are and how they would have been used.

"I'm seriously impressed," Shenna turns a beaming smile on Ryan then turns full circle to take it all in again. "Your students obviously put a lot of effort into this…I could give some really interesting lessons in here then show the children the work you're all doing outside," she tells him with renewed enthusiasm. "I'd keep them at a safe distance," she assures him, "but it would be nice if either yourself or one of the students could answer any questions they might have about the dig process – just a couple of minutes or so?"

Ryan finds himself caught up in her enthusiasm. "I don't see why not – the girls were all for the visitors centre and I'm sure they would be happy to answer any questions." His smile is warm and sincere, his curiosity about Shenna growing by the minute.

You just don't look or sound like the kind of woman that complains unnecessarily or is rude or abusive – maybe Felicity misunderstood.

When they go back outside both of them watch as Neirin, his face a picture of concentration, very carefully scrapes away layers of soil alongside Sadie.

"Your son is very accomplished," Ryan observes not taking his eyes from the small boys actions. "Most children I know wouldn't have the patience or indeed the ability to be so attentively careful."

"He is a joy," Shenna smiles over at her son, her pride and her heart worn openly on her sleeve. "I count my blessings every day – he's the very best part of me and the image of his dad."

Ryan looks sideways to see her expression and isn't surprised to see the love in it. What does surprise him is the twist in his gut, and the admiration he feels for this single mother who appears to be coping wonderfully with the role.

"Do you mind if I ask what happened to your husband?" he asks quietly.

"Cancer happened," she tells Ryan without turning to look at him. "We were trying to start a family a year before I got pregnant with Neirin – we'd just started to get tested for possible fertility problems when the cancer was found."

"I'm sorry," Ryan tells her sincerely, "that must have been hard on you both."

"I found out I was pregnant on the day he died," Shenna's voice is distant with remembering, "and give thanks every day that I did – at least I could give him that one small pleasure."

Swallowing down on his natural response, Ryan fears Shenna might take it as pity and take offence. Instead he focuses on Neirin – a real credit to his mother.

"You've done a fine job with the boy," he tells her as they both watch his total preoccupation with the task in hand. "Neirin has obviously benefitted from being home tutored by an experienced teacher, who just so happens to be his mum."

"I'm sure there are those who would say I was merely selfish," she smiles to herself, "and truth be told, they'd be right."

Neirin's head jerks up and he turns to Sadie – she moves closer and helps him to remove a shard of pottery from the dirt.

"Wow, your first find," Sadie tells him as they very carefully hold it up to examine it closer. Noticing Ryan Tempest and Shenna standing nearby, Sadie holds up the shard to them, "Neirin has found a good piece of pottery – I'll mark the spot and continue searching for the rest," she grins happily

Moving closer, Ryan is pleased to see that the pottery is of the type they are looking for. "Well done, Neirin - if the find is verified as authentic it will be the dig's very first discovery," he tells the boy and watches his grin spread with the excitement of his success. "Sadie will clean this up and catalogue it – then you can add it to the display in the visitors centre with Neirin's name as finder," he tells the young woman crouched at Neirin's side.

"Beginner's luck," Sadie nudges Neirin playfully. "Come with me and I'll show you how to clean this up."

Before leaving Sadie puts a marker in the ground to facilitate the search for more shards to match Neirin's.

"How about a coffee?" Ryan asks Shenna when they are left alone.

"That would be nice," she agrees and they both walk over to his office.

"Well, this looks cosy," Felicity's catty remark precedes her entrance into the port-a-cabin.

Frowning at Felicity's very different tone to the one she used to apologise for the noise nuisance,

Shenna can only wonder what her problem is.

Turning back to Shenna, Ryan says, "I believe you have already met my site coordinator, Felicity Mayfield," he introduces. "And, of course, you have already met Mrs Williams," Ryan narrows his eyes suspiciously at Felicity.

"As I told you," Felicity rounds on him, "not that you seem to care." Before anyone can say anything else she flounces out of the office and across to the port-a-cabin she shares with the other two women.

Shenna stands, looking after the other woman with wide astonished eyes. "That is who I'm meant to have abused?" she asks in a voice thick with disbelief.

Turning back to Shenna, Ryan can see the truth of the matter – in fact, he's had his doubts all along he realises.

"I'm sorry, Felicity has always had a penchant for drama and twisting the truth to suit herself." Having said as much he realises now that it's true. There have been so many times in the past when a member of the team has become upset enough to walk out, and Felicity was never far away.

Maybe it's come time for a parting of the ways. Perhaps, at the end of this dig, I'll just make sure that our paths no longer cross.

When Shenna meets up with her friends Gail and Juliette the next day she tells them about the peculiar incident.

"It was bad enough being woken up at six-thirty in the morning after a very late night of marking and lesson planning – but to then be accused of abusing a member of the dig team was ludicrous and infuriating," Shenna frowns over her mug of tea.

"What did you say – was Neirin with you at the time?" Juliette asks while getting out a packet of ginger biscuits.

"No, thankfully!" Shenna helps herself to a couple of biscuits from the packet that Juliette is holding out to her. "Thanks – at first I was too stunned to say anything but once my brain woke up I was just furious. That's when I marched over to his office and gave him what for."

Gail laughs, "Go Shenna!"

"But I thought he was encouraging you to get involved with the dig – didn't you say that he was actually being nice to you?" Juliette really doesn't understand where the incident has arisen from.

"He was," Shenna replies. "I think that's why I was so stunned when he came to the cottage – it was so out of the blue."

"Do you think this Felicity woman lied to him?" Gail frowns quizzically across the breakfast table at Shenna.

"I think that's quite possible." It's Shenna's turn to frown as she considers Ryan Tempest's reaction to Felicity's sudden appearance and her attitude. "I also think he knows that she lied – or at least, suspects as much." He didn't say that out loud but his expression said it all!

Both of her friends raise their eyebrows at this suggestion.

"But, why would he accuse you if he doesn't even believe her?" Gail is really confused now.

Shaking her head, Shenna explains. "No, I think he really did believe her at that time, but when she stormed into the port-a-cabin yesterday it was like she'd been found out and knew it – though she didn't admit to anything – just flounced out."

"You know," Gail studies her mug of tea, "it sounds like she's jealous."

Choking on the tea she has just sipped, Shenna coughs and splutters while Juliette smacks her smartly on her back.

"Where did that come from?" Shenna asks when she is finally able to speak.

"I told you before that I'd heard they have an on off relationship," Gail reminds her. "What if she wants it to be back on but he isn't cooperating – she might see you as a rival."

Was that it? No...it can't be. It just doesn't make sense!

"Not a chance," Shenna disagrees firmly. "Felicity is beautiful, has a terrific figure and has his occupation in common – they're made for each other."

"Hmm, I think she might agree," Juliette finally joins her friends at the breakfast table with her mug of tea after clearing their lunch dishes away. "After all, we don't know if it was him or her that has made it an on again off again affair – perhaps this time he said enough is enough and means it?"

Nodding enthusiastically, Gail agrees. "And this time he might just be interested in someone else!" Looking over at Juliette they give each other a knowing nod.

"You two are incorrigible," Shenna gapes at their outrageous conclusion. "I know you've tried to fit me up before with 'friends' of your husbands', but this is plain nuts – he hasn't shown the slightest interest and I'd tell him where to go if he did!"

What a pair of matchmakers! And it's not like he's ever said anything or even looked at me funny – they're just wishful thinking.

But her heart has kicked into high gear and her breathing is giving her problems. No. Not a chance.

CHAPTER FIVE

When Ryan examines the find Neirin made recently he feels like he's seen something like it before. But where?

There is only a small amount of the design visible, but it's enough to nag at Ryan as he paws through a catalogue of Roman Britain finds.

"Can I help?" Felicity looks sheepish as she comes into the port-a-cabin looking for Ryan.

Distracted, Ryan looks up, "I've seen this design somewhere – I just can't put my finger on it," he says while turning the shard of pottery in his fingers under a portable magnifying light.

"This is the piece the boy found," Felicity states as she takes the piece from Ryan to examine it. "If I'm not mistaken...," her eyes narrow as she holds the piece under the magnifying light to examine it more closely, "...we have something similar to this on display in the visitors centre...I'm..."

"Bloody hell!" Ryan pushes to his feet and strides out and across to the smaller port-a-cabin. Searching the display he finds what he's looking for in the display of locally found artefacts.

Taking it back to where Felicity stands waiting, Ryan examines the two pieces together and grins widely. "I believe we have a match," he tells her and Felicity beams back at him full of enthusiasm.

"There could be more of it," she tells him. "I know Sadie has been looking in the same spot the boy found that piece," and nods to the shard Ryan is holding in his right hand. "She hasn't found anymore pottery yet but she and Roz have unearthed a couple of coins and a bronze and enamel dragonesque brooch."

Ryan's head flies up, "Why didn't you tell me?" His grin has gone and his eyes narrow on hers.

"For heaven's sakes, Ryan, you only got back this morning," she tells him with a flick of her hand. "The girls are working on cleaning them up and, as you can see, Paul and Carl are still working in the same spot to see what else they can come up with."

"I've been back four hours – you couldn't have found the time to tell me about the finds before this?"

Felicity doesn't answer, just purses her lips and shrugs her shoulders.

"Damn it, Felicity..." Biting back his anger, Ryan decides the less said the better, as he'd only end up saying something he might regret. Instead he strides out and crosses to where the girls are working on the pieces and finds the brooch already cleaned and looking magnificent.

"This is really excellent work," taking out a pocket magnifier, Ryan examines the piece more closely while the two girls give each other an excited thumbs up sign. "How long did it take you to clean?" He looks from one unsure face to another.

"Three days," Sadie grimaces anticipating a telling off for taking so long – that's what they'd received from Felicity just that morning in fact.

"Good," he surprises them and their smiles instantly return. "If you rush these things you're likely to cause irrevocable damage." He moves on to look at the coins, "Another good find," he smiles up at them, "give these the same treatment as the brooch – have the lads found anything?"

The girls grin broadly. "Not yet," and they both give self-congratulatory laughs.

"Ok," Ryan joins in the high spirits, "a bit of competition can be healthy and help relieve the boredom – just don't let it rush your work. Careful digging is the key to finding things and keeping them intact," he reminds them as he leaves.

Getting changed, Ryan decides it's time to get his hands dirty, the best part of the job in his opinion – though he knows Felicity avoids it at all cost. She used to be so enthusiastic – when did the work become just a job to her? I used to love her excitement at finding something new – now she's all about giving orders and sniping at people. She's changed, alright. Shame.

For a couple of hours he works beside Paul and Carl, carefully scraping away the layers of soil around the area of Neirin's find.

Just by chance he looks up as Shenna and Neirin are about to walk away from the taped off boundary line.

"Hey, Neirin," he calls out and brings them both to a stop. Brushing his hands off, Ryan makes his way over and smiles down at the boy. "It's your birthday tomorrow, isn't it?"

Smiling shyly, Neirin nods his head.

"Hmm, thought I'd got it right," Ryan tells him. "I brought you something back with me – want to see it?" Then he looks at Shenna at the same time as Neirin does.

"Ok," she tells them and her ready smile embraces them both.

"Just duck under here and follow me," Ryan holds up the tape for them then leads them over to his office. Sitting at his desk he takes out a canvas roll secured with a tie and hands it over to Neirin. "I'm not big on cards, but I think you'll like this."

Shenna watches as Neirin undoes the tie and lays the roll out flat on Ryan's desk.

Eyes wide with excitement, Neirin looks up at his mum. "Look mum, my very own tools," and shifts his smiling gaze to Ryan. "Thank you so much – will I be able to use them soon?"

Deciding that he's brought it on himself, Shenna leaves Ryan to field that question.

But he doesn't balk at answering and smiles encouragingly at Neirin. "As soon as your mum says you can," and again both sets of eyes fly up to Shenna's.

"Well," taken aback by the jolt her heart gives at

Ryan's sincere enjoyment of Neirin's enthusiasm, and a smile that could melt a polar ice-cap, Shenna finds herself smiling and nodding, "you've already got your play-clothes on, just mind you take care and listen to what Mr Tempest tells you," she warns.

"Ok mum." His smile is the widest she's seen it in a long while.

Such a serious and studious boy, Shenna often worries that he is missing out. It isn't that she has ever pushed Neirin to study as hard as he does; it just seems to be something he enjoys. His mind is like a little sponge that soaks up information and ideas then looks for more.

Ryan stands and seems to take up a lot of room in the port-a-cabin, and Shenna quickly steps outside. "I'll be at the cottage," she tells them both, "so if you want to come home – or you need to get on with other things," she says to Ryan, "just bring Neirin home when you're ready."

Watching her walk back to the cottage, Ryan puts a hand on Neirin's shoulder then urges him over to where the lads are still hard at work.

"I almost forgot," Ryan tells Neirin as he lays out his roll of brand new tools, "we think that pottery piece you found might belong to an earlier find in this area – one of the pieces that brought this dig about in the first place."

"Really!" Neirin is beaming with excitement.

"I'll show you later," Ryan is pleased with the boy's reaction, "for now we need to do some of the boring work."

Eyes wide with shock, Neirin shakes his head, "I don't think it's boring at all – it's exciting."

Giving a laugh that takes even him by surprise, Ryan agrees, "Just what I always say – it's the never knowing what the next scrape of soil is going to reveal that's the joy of this job. Now, let's see what we can find."

Three hours later and Shenna is starting to get just a bit worried. Looking out of her sitting room window she can see the dig site but can't make out individual people through the trees.

She is just about to pull on her shoes and make her way over to see how Neirin is doing when she spots her son and Ryan Tempest coming towards the cottage.

Opening the door before they can knock, Shenna looks down into her son's dirty but happy face.

"We lost track of time," Ryan apologises, "it's my fault Neirin is late."

Frowning curiously up at the tall man at her son's side, Shenna wonders what he expects her to do – shout at Neirin or send him to his room, perhaps.

"I don't think I stipulated a time for Neirin to come home," she tells him, "but if I had I would have walked down to check everything was alright if I were worried."

"Right. Ok then." Looking down at Neirin his smile returns, "Anytime you feel like getting your hands dirty get your mum to bring you down to the site – just check that I'm around," Ryan looks up at Shenna and the smile fades. "Don't just leave him without checking that I'm there – ok?"

Shenna's spine straightens. "I wouldn't dream of leaving my son unattended at the dig site or anywhere else," she tells Ryan in no uncertain terms, her eyes glittering with instant rage.

"You wouldn't be the first to leave a child unattended," he tells her then strides away before she can reply.

"Well!" Hands on hips she huffs loudly, frowning darkly after him. And I was actually starting to like him – what an idiot that makes me! Damn the man! But she can't deny, Ryan is good with Neirin and her son obviously enjoys his company.

"Let's get you in the bath, little man," she smiles down at Neirin and ushers him indoors. "Then we've got ravioli for tea."

Later that evening, when Neirin is in bed and she is relaxing with a glass of white wine, Shenna thinks she hears a noise coming from the back of the cottage but doesn't see anything obvious when she looks out the back window.

Deciding that she's either imagining things or making too much of the wind picking up a piece of debris, Shenna sits back down to continue reading her book.

However, first thing the following morning, Shenna goes out to look in the back garden to see what might have caused the noise she'd heard the night before. Her hand flies up to stifle a scream and avoid waking Neirin as Shenna looks at the body of a badger cub with its little head bashed in. A bloody rock has been left nearby; whoever had done it hadn't even attempted to hide it.

"You poor little thing!" Moving over to get a better look at what some callous person has done to a defenceless creature, Shenna tries to find any tell-tale signs that might tell her who did it.

Bloody coward! Picking on something as

harmless as this is pure cowardice – and why leave it in my back garden?

Moving quickly, Shenna gets a spade and buries the creature before Neirin can see it. She buries the bloody rock nearby too, just in case. What a wretched birthday present that would have been if Neirin had found it! He loves those badgers!

Meeting up with Juliette at Gail's house for the birthday tea she is giving for Neirin and Tommy, Shenna tells them what she found once the boys are outside in the back garden playing.

"Oh god!" Juliette looks at Shenna in disgusted shock. "How could they do that – just bash the poor little things head in?"

Gail comes back in from the kitchen, "I'm more worried about the why than the how," she frowns over at both women sat at her breakfast table drinking the tea she has just made them. "I mean, older kids do these things now and then, we all know that – but why kill it in your back garden and leave it where it's sure to be found?"

Looking through the breakfast room window, Shenna watches Neirin on the climbing frame. "That's been worrying me, too," she admits not taking her eyes off her son. "If Neirin had gone out to the chicken coop to collect the fresh eggs, as he usually does, well…"

"Don't!" Gail warns. "He didn't and that's what you've got to remember. There's no point getting upset by what-if's."

"No, you're right," and Shenna nods her head firmly and turns to her friend. "Would you mind if Neirin has a sleepover with you tonight?"

"Not at all," Gail assures her and is glad to see a weight lift off her friend's shoulders.

"Good. Good." Getting to her feet, Shenna leaves her half-drunk tea and pulls on her cardigan. "I'll just say goodbye to Neirin and then I'm going to get off."

Her two friends watch as Shenna goes outside and gives Neirin the news about the sleepover and a hug goodbye.

"She's really spooked," Juliette tells Gail.

"Wouldn't you be?" Gail asks with raised eyebrows.

Coming back into the breakfast room, Shenna picks up her bag. "I'll give you a ring later," she tells Gail, then says goodbye to Juliette and drives back home.

Sitting outside the cottage in her car she doesn't hear Ryan's approach. He gives a knock on the passenger door window and sees her jump in alarm.

"Are you alright – where's Neirin?" he asks as she steps out of the car and he peers through the rear door window.

"He's having a sleepover with his friend, Tommy – it's his sixth birthday tomorrow so Gail threw them a joint party," she tells him distractedly.

"I asked you if you're alright," Ryan repeats, looking at Shenna with concern, "but you're obviously not – so what's wrong?"

Drawing her gaze from the path that leads to the back of the cottage, Shenna finds herself telling him everything. "I hate to think how Neirin would have reacted if he'd found the badger instead of me. It doesn't bear thinking about."

"Show me." He walks past her down the path and opens the back gate. Shenna follows close behind but he doesn't need her to show him where it happened. The patio has dried from where Shenna had tipped a bucket of water over the blood in an attempt to wash it away, but signs of it still showed in the rough surface of the concrete.

"Do you have a hosepipe?"

Startled by his abrupt request Shenna springs into action to retrieve it from the garden shed. "This should do it," and hands him the length of hose with an attachment for the outside tap at one end and an adjustable nozzle at the other, "I just didn't think." Her hands lift and fall in a helpless gesture.

"Don't worry about it," he tells her and proceeds to thoroughly hose the patio down. Turning off the tap he carefully winds up the hose and ties it with the cloth she uses to secure it in the shed. He turns the key in the lock and returns it to Shenna. "Any idea who might have done it – some tearaway kids, perhaps?"

Shaking her head she looks up at him, her green eyes baffled. "I've racked my brain and can't think of anyone. I don't know of any child, boy or girl, who would be capable of doing such a thing – and I'm certainly not aware of anyone who would have a reason to do it in my back garden. I mean...why?" she asks him totally confused.

An imposing figure, Ryan stands tall at six feet four. Surveying the surrounding area he asks Shenna who would know that Neirin likes to collect the eggs from the chicken coop.

"You think this was aimed at Neirin?" Her cheeks pale and one hand covers her heart, the other reaches out for something to steady her, then Shenna finds herself being steadied by Ryan himself. Hands on his broad chest she looks up with frightened eyes at the man holding her.

"Don't panic...I just thought it might be a boy that Neirin has told about the chickens and the fact that he regularly collects the eggs." Turning her about, Ryan puts a supporting arm round her shoulders and guides her to the front door. He holds out a large hand palm up, "Keys!"

Without a second thought Shenna hands them over and finds herself being helped inside and onto the settee.

Her stillness is what worries Ryan. He strides down the lounge to find the kitchen and comes back a couple of minutes later with a mug of tea. "Here...drink this."

Sat exactly where he'd left her, Shenna looks up to see Ryan offering her the mug. Taking it automatically, she cradles it in her hands resting on her knees and thanks him.

"Did your mother teach you to make tea in a crisis?" she asks, but cringes back into the settee at the look he gives her.

"My mother didn't teach me anything," he replies brusquely. "Her Johns, however, were sometimes quite informative."

Her mouth falls open but no words come out.

"Yes, even prostitutes have children," he growls at the memory of his childhood.

"I don't know whether to be sorry or not," she whispers. "Not all prostitutes are necessarily bad parents."

He lowers his eyes and shakes his head giving a wry smile, "Well, this one was – her idea of a treat was remembering to leave me something to eat before she went out walking the streets."

Why the bloody hell am I telling her any of this? Still, looks like it's brought some colour back into her cheeks!

"Forget about that," he dismisses with a flick of his large hand, "you are going to be on your own here tonight – is that right?"

Shenna nods, not sure where the conversation is going now.

He nods and considers for a moment. "I could ask one or both of the female students to stay over with you," he offers and studies her reaction keenly.

Now she thought about it, the idea of being in the house on her own tonight wasn't at all appealing, but she didn't want to admit that.

"I'll be fine," Shenna shakes her head and takes a

gulp of hot tea. Swallowing quickly, she coughs then takes another sip to sooth her throat. "I'm sure it was just a one-off prank."

He can see that she isn't at all sure of that but doesn't push the matter. "Just make sure you lock up tight and don't go outside even if you do hear something." Then he hands her a business card after underlining one of the numbers on it. "That's my mobile – call if you hear anything at all."

Still sitting stunned on the settee, Shenna finds herself suddenly alone.

He's like a one man tornado – I've never felt so spun around!

But it isn't just his take charge manner that has put her head in a spin. Even half out of her mind with worry for Neirin she had been aware of the man holding her to him in the garden. His body had felt warm and hard beneath her palms. She had felt his heart beat regular and strong, and his lungs expand his impressive chest with each breath.

Her body gives an involuntary quiver.

Just tension. Nothing to do with Ryan Tempest – he's just got me all turned around, no more than that.

But she dreams of him that night. He is beside her and she has her hands on his chest only this time there is nothing covering his hot flesh. She feels his hands on her, her nipples ripening to his touch – and then he is inside her, pushing deeply, slowly…

"I can't," she cries out into the empty bedroom and sits up when she hears a noise outside the cottage. Getting up quickly, Shenna pulls on a robe and crosses to look out of the front window. She can't see anything but decides to check out of Neirin's window which overlooks the back garden.

"Oh lord!" A shadow is moving about; she doesn't have one of those automatic security lights but vows to get one fitted the very next day – but for now she is on her own and someone is prowling around.

Then she remembers the card that Ryan had given her and creeps downstairs to get it. Dialling the number she hears his deep voice come awake quickly, "What's wrong?" he asks without her saying a word.

"Someone's in the back garden," she whispers trying not to sound as frightened as she really is.

"I'm on my way!"

Looking at the phone in surprise she puts it back in its cradle then moves to the sitting room window to watch for Ryan.

She sees his large form move up the dark path and go to the side of the house. He is going straight to the back garden she realises, and runs to the back door.

This is her problem; she can't let him face some maniac on his own – though what she can do to help him is anyone's guess.

Picking up her keys she slides back the bolt and lets herself out of the back door. Just as she does so a shadow pushes past her and runs off into the bushes. Hearing a groan Shenna hurries out in her bare feet to see what has happened.

Ryan is holding his stomach and his head is bleeding.

"Oh my lord, Ryan," she hurries over and kneels beside him. "What did they do to you...your head is bleeding...oh heck...this is my stupid fault, I should never have called you!"

"I'll be alright," he growls, angry at himself for letting whoever it was get the drop on him. "Just give me a hand to get up."

She tries to help him balance as he sways to his feet, and then helps him into the house through the kitchen and onto the settee in the sitting room.

"Lock the back door!" His voice is hard and

stinging, but she says nothing and moves to do as she's been told.

When she comes back Ryan is looking at his blood smeared hand having wiped it over the back of his head.

"Let me look at that," she tells him, recovering some of her own equilibrium. Moving to stand in front of him, Shenna urges him to drop his head forward so that she can examine the back of his head. "It needs cleaning – just stay there and I'll get a bowl and the first aid kit."

Ryan feels giddy and he's not entirely sure it's down to the blow on his head. She had smelt good standing so near to him – all female and sexy. Her robe had fallen open and her silky nightdress had brushed his cheek as she leaned over him.

He hadn't been tended by a woman in years and then it had been a nurse just doing her job when he'd had his arm slashed in a street fight as a teenager.

Standing in front of him, Shenna sets a bowl on a nearby table, then opens the substantial first aid kit to reveal all manner of dressings and bandages.

He frowns into the box then up at Shenna. "You do this sort of thing often?"

Cocking her head to one side with an eyebrow

raised, Shenna simply states, "I have a son who lives in a forest and loves to climb and run – so yes, this lot comes in very handy on a fairly regular basis."

His full lips pull into a grin that holds her mesmerised. "I suppose so," he nods and remembers skinning his own knees a time or two as a lad. But there had been no caring mother to clean him up and tend his scrapes – he'd taken care of himself, as always.

Bending as low as he can to allow her access, Ryan can't help breathing in the scent of her again and finds it difficult to reign in his imagination. She might be a widow and a single mother, but she is also a young attractive woman with needs and he can imagine himself fulfilling them.

As soon as she's finished Ryan pushes up and strides over to the door.

"Thanks," he clears his throat and tries to avert his eyes from her barely concealed breasts. "Make sure you lock up after I've gone – I doubt they'll have the nerve to hang around but stay inside with everywhere locked up tight just in case!"

Then he was gone. Again! What is it about my house that causes him to run out of it? He didn't even give me a chance to thank him, damn it! Now I suppose I'll have to go over to the dig site in the morning. Remembering his injuries she realises that she would have done that anyway.

CHAPTER SIX

With her internet and skype connection back up and running, Shenna has a lot of teaching to catch up on.

Time flies by and with no further incidents life settles back into its old routine. The only change to that routine is the regular time Neirin spends at the dig site.

Thankfully Ryan Tempest hadn't suffered any ill effects from the attack that had taken place in her own back garden – though she's sure his pride had taken an even bigger knock than his head. He hadn't been too pleased when she'd gone to check up on him the following morning and had refused to let her examine him to make sure the injury to his head was clean and had not become infected.

Going upstairs to fetch some notes ready for her next skype enabled lesson, Shenna stops outside of Neirin's bedroom and listens to him talking. She is just about to walk quietly away when Neirin comes to the door.

"Hi," he smiles up at her, "can I go to the dig today?"

Shenna gives him a playful frown, "Can you go to the dig today?" Giving him a second or two to think about what he has said, Shenna chuckles. "You can go to the dig but whether or not you may go is another matter – don't you think?"

Her five year old son actually rolls his eyes at her and Shenna has a hard time keeping a straight face.

"May I go to the dig today please," he asks with studied care.

"You may," she smiles and gives him a hug. "Just let me get Jenna's study papers and I'll walk you over. But remember," She turns back to him, "you can't stay unless Mr Tempest is there."

"He's there," Neirin states confidently and goes to turn away, but Shenna stops him with a curious look. "Dad told me, Ryan came back an hour ago."

Watching as her son goes back into his bedroom to change into his play clothes, Shenna stands speechless and shocked.

I thought he was over this…he hasn't mentioned talking with his dad for over a week now. And since when has Mr Tempest become Ryan!

Walking with Neirin through the trees to the dig site, Shenna tries not to show how troubled she is by this latest development. But when Ryan steps out of his port-a-cabin he takes one look at her face and knows something is wrong.

"Is it alright?" Neirin asks and Ryan nods knowing exactly what he means.

"Go over to Sadie and Roz, they found another piece of your pot this morning – see if you can find some more." He watches the boy stride off happily then turns to his mother. "What's wrong – have you had another incident without calling me?!"

He looks and sounds angry. Just hold the phone, big guy – I've been looking after myself for a long time now.

To Ryan she says, "If I had had another incident it isn't for you to worry about. I am a very capable woman and Neirin and I have managed just fine for a very long time now."

Pulling in a heavy breath Ryan watches her distracted expression and the way her eyes keep flicking over to Neirin. The boy is safe and sound enjoying himself yet his mother is watching him like a hawk.

"Come inside and have a coffee with me," he offers and turns without waiting for her answer.

Torn, Shenna watches Neirin for a moment longer then follows in Ryan's wake.

"Did you go somewhere this morning – or come back from being away from the site overnight?" Shenna watches as he finishes pouring two mugs of filter coffee from the jug and steps towards her to hand her one. "I mean, maybe he saw you come back...Neirin...maybe he saw you come back and that's how he knew you were here – right?"

Ryan holds a hand out toward a chair and asks her to sit down. "Now tell me what's troubling you and what it's got to do with me being away from the dig site this morning."

Watching him over her mug Shenna frowns and tries not to freak out. "When did you get back?" Please don't say an hour ago, I don't think my head can take anymore of this weirdness.

Looking at his watch Ryan considers, "A little over an hour ago, why?"

As her hands begin to shake Shenna's coffee comes perilously close to spilling. Ryan springs up and takes the mug before she can come to any harm.

"Will you just tell me what the hell is going on?"

Feeling dizzy Shenna closes her eyes and the next thing she feels is a hand on the back of her head pushing it down to her knees. She stays there for a minute and annoyingly does feel a bit better.

"Ok, ok," she tells him as she pushes herself upright, "I'm fine...I'm ok, really," she tells him when he only frowns sceptically at her. Picking up her coffee she takes a sip and begins to normalise. "I just had a bit of a shock, that's all. It's nothing."

Watching her try to dismiss the incident only annoys him further. "This obviously involves Neirin – are you unhappy that he enjoys spending time here? Or perhaps it's the amount of time he's spending here?"

Shenna looks up quickly. "Is he outstaying his welcome – I didn't realise...I'll try to rein him in."

Now he is angry. "Don't you turn this on me!" He stands and actually manages a short pace back and forth in what little space the port-a-cabin affords. "You are one infuriating woman! Why can't you just come out with whatever is troubling you, I might ev..."

"Neirin talks to his dad," she blurts out then

blows out a long breath and watches the significance of what she has said actually dawn on him. "Yes...exactly!"

"Are you saying that he has conversations with his dead father – or is he talking in his sleep?"

"I wouldn't be worried about him talking in his sleep," she replies, then stands and moves over to the door to watch Neirin scraping away carefully at the soil. "He's such a loving soul. He doesn't whine like other children wanting this or that and he rarely has a tantrum," forgetting herself she turns a smile on Ryan that has him catching his breath, "but when he does you'd better duck for cover – I suppose a good mad is just his way of letting off steam now and then."

Turning back to watch Neirin, Shenna has no idea of the effect she's having on Ryan.

What is it that's worrying you so much...the fact that your son believes he can talk to his dad...or the thought that your dead husband might be haunting you?

"Does Neirin appear to be upset by the situation in any way?" Ryan asks quietly.

"No...no he doesn't," Shenna walks back and sits down to her coffee. "He just seems to think its normal, nothing worrying about it."

"Then why are you?" Ryan watches her intently, unsure how he feels about her dead husband hanging around.

Eyebrows raised Shenna looks at Ryan in surprise. "Wouldn't you be – if Neirin were your son, wouldn't you be worried about him?"

Surprised by the sudden stab of longing at the mention of Neirin, Ryan considers then nods in agreement. "I suppose I would, but couldn't it be just another version of the invisible friend that lots of children imagine at his age?"

"I've thought of that and wished fervently that it were." Shenna looks over at Ryan, her green eyes filled with love and concern for her son. "But that doesn't explain how he knew you were back – knew, Ryan, for a certainty that you were back on site and when you came back."

"Ok, I admit that's a puzzle," Ryan concedes, "but couldn't he have just seen my car drive onto the site. Is there a window, other than your bedroom window, that looks out towards the dig site?"

He knows which room my bedroom is! How does he know that – does he watch the lights go out when I go to bed? I suppose that could be it...

"I...yes...the landing window," she confirms

pulling her wayward thoughts back on track, "but that wasn't it. Neirin was studying in his room and only came out just before we came down here. I was searching upstairs for some study papers for Jaden when he came out and asked me if he could come to the site – I said yes as long as Mr Tempest is there...and he said 'he is there, dad told me Ryan came back an hour ago', then he just went back into his room to change. Just like that...," and she lifts her hands palms up and lets them fall into her lap, "...as if he's just told me about a conversation he had with Tommy or one of his other friends."

"Mum look!" A very excited Neirin is standing at the doorway with Sadie, holding a substantial piece of pottery in his little hands. His eyes shift to look at Ryan and his smile widens even more, "Sadie and Roz think it belongs to the other pieces," and he holds it out for Ryan to look at.

Having moved to the door, Ryan takes the piece that Neirin is holding out to him and moves over to the table top magnifying lamp to examine it more carefully.

Neirin climbs the steps and follows him, biting his bottom lip now in anticipation.

Shenna is fascinated by the bond that has sprung

up between the two and is glad that Neirin has a man in his life that he can look up to, for however brief a time.

Apart from being a bit overbearing and sometimes arrogant, you are a good man, I'm sure of that. You certainly care about Neirin and that counts for a lot in my book!

Switching off the lamp, Ryan turns an approving smile on Neirin and gives him a confirmation nod. "Did you dig this up?" he asks and his smile brightens when Neirin nods enthusiastically. "Well you did a good job – there are no tool marks on here so you must have been very careful when you did it. Did Sadie and Roz help?"

Neirin bites his lip and flicks a glance at Sadie still waiting outside the doorway, then nods reluctantly.

"Good, that's why you work with them," Ryan tells the boy. "This is important work, Neirin – we're finding out about the lives of people who lived hundreds of years ago, right here in your forest."

His face alive with interest, Neirin takes back the piece of pottery he found. "Sadie said to imagine another little boy holding this pot for his mum and that now I'm holding it after all this time!" His eyes were large and round at the thought and Shenna didn't think she'd seen him so entranced by anything she'd ever taught him.

"Sadie is exactly right," Ryan agrees looking over at the girl. "And that's what archaeology is all about. It's why it is so exciting and compelling – once you start finding things and putting them all together to build up a picture of what life was like back then, the more you want to find and begin to feel a part of that past."

Nodding in earnest, Neirin simply said, "Yes, like my fingers touching the same place as that other boy."

When Neirin returns to Sadie she takes him to put the pottery piece safely away and then returns to their digging.

Standing, Shenna walks over to the door then looks back at Ryan. "I can't thank you enough for what you and your crew have given Neirin," she tells him sincerely. "He'll never forget what you have taught him, or your friendship, I think."

Finding it difficult to think of not seeing Neirin again, Ryan frowns and tries to dismiss the feelings he has for the boy. "It's been my pleasure."

"Yes, I believe you mean that." Then Shenna is gone, having waved to her son she is striding off towards the cottage before Ryan can think of anything else to say.

Through the visitors centre window, Felicity has watched the exit of Shenna Williams with interest. Her son is spending a lot of time at the dig – she can't stand children so makes sure she is out of the way when he is around. For a moment she watches the boy with Sadie and Roz then gives a dismissive growl and returns to cataloguing and displaying the recent finds.

Having trouble concentrating on her teaching session, Shenna is annoyed with herself for allowing thoughts of Ryan Tempest to distract her. When it is finished she decides that a trip into town is warranted, they are running low on a few things and a trip to the supermarket might clear her head.

First she needs to go over to the dig to let them know she won't be home. Either Neirin can stay a while longer or she can take him home to change and he can go with her to the supermarket.

"No problem," Ryan assures her, brushing the dirt off his hands as he stands to talk to her. "It'll be easier for you to get your shopping done alone and Neirin is fine here."

Her son looks up and nods in agreement then

wipes a filthy hand across his cheek to leave a smear of dirt to add to the others he's got streaked over his face.

Thinking of a saying her mum used to tell her dad when she came in mucked up from playing, 'a mucky child is a happy child' Shenna turns to leave, knowing her son is happy and safe.

The supermarket is busy; Shenna strolls up and down the aisles putting this and that into her trolley then is surprised by someone talking to her from behind.

"The dig site isn't a nursery for your convenience," Felicity tells her with a snarl in her voice.

Turning in surprise to face the obviously annoyed woman, Shenna doesn't let her rile her. "Really, but it's so handy," she replies sarcastically. I shouldn't have said that. Damn it!

"You're pathetic," Felicity sneers, "throwing yourself at Ryan, trying to find a father for that brat – you couldn't be more pathetic."

Putting Neirin into the mix was a mistake and Shenna's spine straightens immediately. "If you have a problem with Neirin being at the dig site take it up with Ryan, he seems quite happy for him to be there."

Giving a derogatory laugh Felicity gives Shenna a pitying look. "You really don't get it do you? Ryan and I are an item, I don't want kids but he does so he's enjoying yours for a while – that's all!"

Shocked that Ryan would still be involved with a woman who is obviously so cold and selfish, Shenna can't reconcile that fact with the image of the man she had spoken with that morning.

"I'm not throwing myself at Ryan or anyone else," Shenna states firmly. "Neirin and I have a very full life together, he doesn't need a man in his life but if he's enjoying Ryan's company then I won't stop him." And neither will you!

After putting all the groceries away Shenna has a teaching session with Neirin's friend, Tommy. He is coming along so much now; his confidence is growing by the day. It's the part of teaching that she loves, to see a child who once believed he was 'thick' and 'stupid' come as far as Tommy has is payment in itself. His behaviour at home has improved too – he used to have a very short fuse on his temper, but now he's really laid back and has found his sense of humour again.

Over the next couple of weeks things go from bad to worse, and reach a point where Shenna is actually afraid for Neirin's safety. She has tried to avoid being alone with Ryan after the unpleasant run-in she'd had with his site coordinator, Felicity Mayfield.

That anyone might think she is chasing after Ryan is bad enough, that they think she is trying to snare a father for her child is mortifying. But now she has to put her child's safety before her own pride.

Knocking on the door of Ryan's port-a-cabin office, Shenna steps inside when she hears his abrupt, "In."

Wondering if she's doing the right thing Shenna stands quietly for a moment watching Ryan examining an object under the magnifying lamp.

Without looking up he snaps, "What."

"I can see you're busy," Shenna turns to the door and starts to step through it, "I'll come back another time."

Ryan's head snaps up, she is the reason he's been in a bad mood lately – one because he hasn't been able to get her out of his head, two because she's obviously been avoiding him and he can't think why and three because he hasn't been able to get her out of his head! Damn it!

"Wait!" He continues to look at the metal object that has just been unearthed from the site, but now he's just stalling for time to compose himself.

Coming to stand at his desk, Shenna begins to feel stupid for even being there. Why did I think he would even care – except that Neirin is involved and I know he genuinely cares for him? Yes, I have to put Neirin's safety first!

"Take a seat, will you have some coffee?" he offers stiffly.

Shenna nods and sits, "Thank you."

When they are both settled with their coffee the silence is tangible, deafening.

"I...I'm not sure that I should be here," Shenna begins nervously.

"Why don't you start with what brought you here and we'll take it from there." His voice has softened but there's still an edge of annoyance to it.

"There have been some more incidents at the cottage and I'm becoming worried for Neirin's safety," she tells him then drags in a huge breath and lets it out slowly in an effort to calm herself. "I realise this is not your problem but..."

"What exactly has happened?"

Shenna gives a shudder inside, his tone has become dangerous and she's sure that, contrary to outward appearances, he's furious inside.

"Well...there have been more dead animals," she tells him and watches a tell-tale nerve give a twitch under his right eye, "but it's more the way they were killed that's gotten me worried...and the messages..." she tails off when his expression goes from hard and cold to hot and now openly angry.

"Messages...?" he explodes. "So it's gone from some anonymous idiot trying to scare you to actually making contact," his glittering blue eyes have darkened dangerously, "and you've left it till now to come and tell me, why?"

Trying to stiffen her spine and take back a little bit of control, Shenna lifts her chin defiantly, "Because me and mine are not your concern!" So stop trying to intimidate me!

"You let some idiotic notion of standing on your own two feet stop you from coming to me?" His brow is deeply furrowed and his voice has gone quiet – though Shenna takes no comfort from that. "You put your pig-headed pride in front of Neirin's safety...unbelievable!"

She wanted to tell him that he was wrong but, now Shenna thought about it, she knew he was basically right. "I didn't realise that's what I was doing," she gives a deflating sigh and rubs both hands over her face, "but you're right...I should have come to you sooner."

Her uncharacteristic capitulation is his undoing. Ryan's temper cools as quickly as it flared and he retakes his seat. "Why have you been avoiding me?"

Feeling the colour rise in her cheeks Shenna opens her mouth to deny it then sees the glint of anger still in his eyes. "I didn't want to add fuel to the gossip."

"Gossip!" Well, he hadn't been expecting that. "What gossip?"

"That I'm chasing after you to get a new father for my son!" Her embarrassment is causing her own anger to start boiling up.

He looks at her steadily then says just one word. "Felicity!"

Scowling Shenna tells him that he obviously knows her well. "She made her feelings known when I was in the supermarket – the day I left Neirin here at your suggestion."

Thumping the desk in front of him Ryan gets up to pace again. "Damn that woman!" He walks to the door and back again. "I can't see her just now but believe me I'll be having a word." Pushing his hands back through his blond hair, Ryan tries to calm down. "Tell me about the messages – what did they say?"

"They were very succinct, just 'LEAVE' in block capitals, but were all written in the animal's own blood using a twig or some such object."

"Did Neirin see any of them?"

Shenna rubbed a hand over her tired eyes, she hasn't been sleeping very well – almost waiting for the next thing to happen and had been afraid that things might escalate.

"He doesn't know anything – I get up at six each morning and clear whatever it is away." Shenna looks at him with such concern in her eyes that the last of Ryan's temper eases away. "The last animal, a squirrel, was left hanging by the neck in a make-shift noose," a tear falls unheeded onto her now pale cheek, "it had Neirin's name on the note that was pinned to it." She covers her trembling lips with an equally trembling hand. "I don't know what to do...if I've done something to upset someone and Neirin gets hurt I'll never forgive myself."

Ryan moves swiftly round the desk and pulls her up and into his strong, protective arms. Laying her cheek against his chest, Shenna allows herself to take some comfort.

"Stop worrying," Ryan soothes against her hair, "we won't let anything happen to Neirin." Just let the bastard try – they'll have to get through me first!

"I don't know what we can do...I've racked my brain to think who it could be but I have no idea."

Reluctantly holding her away from him, Ryan looks down in to her tear filled eyes - so green, almost fairy-like and hypnotising. "I want you to go back there," and he points to the rear of the port-a-cabin, which is the male sleeping quarters, and to a sink on the right hand wall, "get freshened up then take Neirin home – I've only got a couple of things that I need to do first then I'll come up to the cottage and we'll talk – ok?"

Nodding, Shenna blinks back the tears in her eyes and tries to smile, "Thank you, I'm sorry I cried all over you," and she lifts a still trembling hand to point at the damp patch on his shirt.

Giving a chuckle Ryan dismisses the damage easily, "My pleasure, I assure you," he tells her. "Any man would welcome the job of comforting a beautiful woman now and then."

Her head tilts to one side to consider this complicated man. One minute he's arrogant and demanding the next he's obliging and accommodating, she just doesn't know who the real Ryan Tempest is.

"Well, thank you again...for me and for Neirin," then she turns towards the sink and freshens up as he suggested.

Leaving her alone, Ryan goes to speak to Felicity. After a few minutes of looking he has to conclude that she isn't on site but he'll make a point of finding her later. We need to talk Felicity and I'm going to make damned sure that we do!

"Neirin," he calls out to the concentrating boy, and his head lifts to look expectantly at him, "your mum is in my office – go and say hello, I'll be in in a minute."

"Ok," Neirin gives Ryan a beaming smile and brushes his hands against each other to dust them off, then walks to the port-a-cabin.

To Sadie and Roz, Ryan says, "Where's Felicity, I can't find her on site?"

The girls look at each other and both shake their heads and shrug their shoulders. "I don't remember seeing her since mid-morning," Roz states.

"Yes that's right," Sadie agrees, "she told us to clean the displays around tenish," she looks up to Ryan, "I don't remember seeing her since then either."

"Is something wrong?" Roz asks.

"No, but I could have done with letting her know that I'll be away from site myself overnight."

"We can tell her when she gets back," Sadie offers cheerfully.

"If you're sure," Ryan falters and frowns down at the girls. "I want you girls to stay on site while I'm away - if Paul and Carl are planning to go out this evening, tell them I'd rather they didn't and I'll speak to you all tomorrow – ok?"

Confused and curious both girls nod in unison and Ryan heads over to the port-a-cabin. When he gets there he finds Shenna doing her best to explain why Neirin has to go home with her earlier than was planned, but the little boy isn't very happy about it.

"That's enough, Neirin," he tells the boy quietly as he steps through the door behind him, "if your mum says it's time to go you pack up quietly and leave – understand."

For the first time since he's known Neirin, Ryan sees the beginnings of a temper brewing.

"But I've been helping Sadie and Roz and I haven't been naughty so why do I have to go home?" Arms folded across his chest he frowns over at his mum defiantly.

As intelligent as the little boy is that is exactly

what he still is, a little boy and one who feels particularly hard done by.

Ryan ruffles his hair, "You haven't done anything wrong Neirin, but your mum needs to take you home." Looking at Shenna he continues, "If you're ready to go I can come up with you now – that business I was going to take care of can wait till later."

Neirin's face goes from crestfallen to excited in a millisecond. "You're coming home with us...," he asks then looks towards his mum for confirmation, "...for tea...are you coming for tea?" his head whips back round to stare wide eyed up at Ryan.

Ryan looks over at Shenna and she gives him a nod, then he smiles down at Neirin and passes the nod along. "Looks like it."

No longer reluctant, Neirin heads for the door and down the steps then waves over at Sadie and Roz. "Bye...Ryan is coming home for tea."

The girls' eyebrows go up but they just wave as the three of them move off.

After their meal, Ryan sits listening to Neirin read while Shenna clears the pots away in the dishwasher and wipes down the kitchen. In the doorway she stands watching them, her son so fluent and proud, Ryan listening attentively.

For a moment her heart fills with what ifs. This is how it should have been with Cade and Neirin and me. You've missed so much Cade and so has Neirin.

At that moment, with her heart worn so plainly on her sleeve, Ryan looks up and sees Shenna's pain. Bloody hell!

"Time for your bath, little man," Shenna pulls on a bright smile for her son.

He is just about to protest when he remembers the warning that Ryan had given him earlier. "Ok, I'm coming," and reluctantly closes the book and wiggles down off the settee. "Goodnight, Ryan."

"Goodnight Neirin," Ryan smiles fondly at the boy.

After tucking Neirin into bed and reading him a story Shenna returns to Ryan in the sitting room.

"He fell asleep before the end of the story," she tells Ryan with a doting smile and crosses the room to the kitchen. Coming to the doorway she holds up half a bottle of red and an unopened bottle of white wine. "I'm going to have a glass of wine; I have red or white if you'd like to join me?"

"A glass of red would be nice," he replies and watches her turn back into the kitchen.

When Shenna reappears she is holding two

almost full glasses of red wine. "I thought we might as well polish it off," she explains, handing Ryan his wine.

Taking a sip Ryan gives an approving nod. "This is good," he tells her and takes another sip before placing the glass on a small table at the side of the settee.

"Mmm...," Shenna smiles appreciatively after taking a sip of her wine, "...I don't indulge very often but when I do I like something decent."

Moving to the nearby armchair Shenna takes a seat drawing her legs up under her and begins to feel awkward.

After a minute or two of silence Ryan decides to get the ball rolling. "When did you find the last animal – the squirrel with Neirin's name pinned to it?"

Giving an involuntary shudder at the memory Shenna tells him everything. "This morning, and it was the most shocking of all – it was pinned so that when I opened the front door it was there in my face," she grimaces and shudders again. "Its belly was cut down the middle and its innards had been deliberately pulled out on display – I just hope the poor creature was dead before that happened." If

Neirin had seen one of his squirrel friends strung up like that he would have been traumatised for sure!

"Have you kept any of the notes?"

Shenna closes her eyes and shakes her head. "I should have shouldn't I – but I was afraid Neirin might come across them."

"Hmm..." Ryan contemplates, "...you're right, of course – but if you could save the next one – and there will be a next one," he warns gravely, "perhaps you could have an envelope at the ready to seal it in and then pass it on to me as soon as possible."

Frowning in confusion Shenna asks, "What are you planning to do with it – I didn't see any distinguishing marks on the paper. They were all the same, just plain scraps of paper."

"I have friends in useful places," he tells her mysteriously, "and I'm owed a few favours – I'm going to be calling a couple of them in to get the note analysed forensically."

With her green eyes popping, Shenna almost chokes on the wine she is sipping. "Good lord, I had no idea – but it sounds brilliant!"

"Good, I was hoping you'd approve," Ryan nods and smiles. "Have you had any more thoughts about who could be behind it all?"

"Not really – just a few disgruntled parents to do with my home tutoring," she shrugs.

"How disgruntled, and what were they disgruntled about?"

"Well, I suppose a couple of the parents were quite upset when I told them that I couldn't take their children on for home tutoring," she recalls. "But apart from the initial calls demanding explanations and then pleading their case, I haven't heard from either family since."

"Any others – perhaps someone who was a bit more threatening?"

"Actually...," Shenna frowns with concentration, "...Mr Carson, the father of one of the pupils I had to let go, became very abusive on the telephone, but I can't say he was threatening...not specifically."

"You said 'one of the pupils you had to let go', who else was there?" Ryan leans forward in his seat, feeling for the first time that they are getting somewhere.

"There were three pupils," she tells him, "all of them caught cheating on multiple occasions and after being warned what would happen if it continued."

"How long ago?"

She considers, "Hmm, about eight months ago –

Catherine Carson, Sally Hampton and Craig Sandyforth." Taking another sip of her wine, Shenna's eyes narrow. "Now I think of it, Mr Sandyforth was a little threatening – he did say that if I found my tyres slashed and my car covered in paint then I would know who it was and to expect worse if I put it about that his son was a cheat."

It is Ryan's turn to look wide-eyed. "And you didn't think of him until now – he was openly hostile and made actual threats?"

Shaking her head and smiling at his affront on her behalf, Shenna explains. "As a teacher I've heard all kinds of threats over the years – it's par for the course," she tells him without concern. "Every parent who thinks little Johnny should have got an A instead of a C- complains in one way or another – if we took them all seriously we'd be basket cases."

For the next couple of hours they talk easily, slipping from the serious topic of the dead animals into small talk about their careers and how they had gotten to their present situations.

They learned a lot about each other and were able to laugh at some of the bumps they'd taken along the road. Then Shenna noticed the time and points it out to Ryan.

"It's quarter to eleven," she tells him, amazed that the evening has passed so quickly, "I didn't mean to keep you so late."

At first Ryan doesn't say anything, just contemplates Shenna and his plan to stay the night. "I'm staying, Shenna...," he watches her mouth drop open then close and draw her bottom lip between her teeth, "...I'm not leaving you and Neirin on your own with some idiot on the loose, out to get their kicks by leaving you dead animals. I'll be comfortable on there," and waves a hand toward the settee.

Drawing in a breath and letting out a deep sigh, Shenna looks at Ryan with troubled eyes. "I ought to protest but the truth is I'm actually relieved at the thought of you being here," she admits with a rueful smile then looks at the settee and back to Ryan. "You're very tall," she observes with concern, "I'm not sure you will fit on the settee – why don't I..."

"No," he dismisses the idea before she can properly voice it. "I'll be fine and I want to be downstairs so that I can hear anything going on and have a chance at catching them!"

Remembering the last time he tried to catch the perpetrator Shenna once again looks troubled.

"What now?" Ryan asks patiently.

"I...well...you got hurt the last time you tangled with them – I don't want you to take any chances." *I can't bear to think of you getting hurt like that again.*

Watching her Ryan has to hold himself in check – he wants nothing more than to take her in his arms and kiss away all the worry he can see on her lovely face, and his gut is twisting at the thought.

Shenna can see his torment but not the reason for it.

"Stop worrying about me and go get a good night's sleep," he tells her and shoves his hands in his pockets as Shenna makes to pass him so as not to reach out and hold her as he wants to.

"I'll bring you some bedding down," she smiles over at him nervously as she starts up the stairs.

As she gathers sheets, pillows and a quilt together, Shenna feels her stomach lurch and her breathe catch at the thought of Ryan spending the night under her roof. *Not that it means anything – he's just worried about Neirin, that's all. And it's not like I want it to mean anything or, at least...I don't think I do!*

CHAPTER SEVEN

"Marry you!" Shenna almost screams her response to Ryan's proposal. "Are you out of your mind – you spend one night sleeping on my settee and now you want to marry me...why?!"

"I need a wife, you need a husband and more importantly Neirin needs a father," Ryan states almost businesslike.

"My son needs me," Shenna frowns resentful of Ryan's assertions. "I've taken care of Neirin just fine up to now, why do you suddenly feel that I'm not up to the job?"

Putting a mug of coffee in front of Ryan on the breakfast table, Shenna takes her own mug to sit opposite him.

"Circumstances have changed," he tells her

calmly, his deep brown voice full of reason. "I've looked outside, there are no dead animals and no sign of an intruder – a man's presence is a deterrent on many levels – you'll both be safer with me around."

Damn it...I did sleep better last night...the best I have in weeks...but that's no reason to marry someone!

But the reason she had slept so well was because she hadn't been worrying about Neirin's safety, she finally admitted to herself.

Ryan watches her thoughts and sees that Shenna is wavering.

"You know it makes sense," Ryan urges gently. "Neirin would hate moving away from here and these past few weeks have shown you just how vulnerable you both are." Watching her green eyes study him, he can see the answer he wants pushing to the surface. "Marry me, Shenna, I'll look after you and Neirin...he won't want for anything."

This is crazy! Just plain crazy! But he means it...and Neirin loves him...

Before she fully realises what she's doing Shenna's head begins a slow nod. I love you Cade...but we need Ryan...

Standing, Ryan walks around to stand in front of Shenna and, taking her hands, gently pulls her to her feet.

Being so close to him makes Shenna tremble. Is that fear or lust!

As his mouth descends Shenna's mind goes into a spin – it's been years since a man kissed her and the fire of his breath against her lips is so good.

This shouldn't be happening...shouldn't be...oh god, you smell so damn good...taste so...

There is no fighting it, she goes under for the third time and drowns in his passion. He ignites in her something she has long thought of as dead and buried along with Cade – but this is different, Ryan is setting alight new fires in her body, exciting her with just his lips and making her want so much more.

"Mummy?"

They spring apart and stand staring at Neirin in the kitchen doorway, and he is smiling.

"Does this mean you're going to be my new daddy?" he asks Ryan directly.

"Would you mind if it did?" he asks Neirin and waits with bated breath for his answer.

But Neirin doesn't say anything, just lunges forward with his arms open and hugs Ryan hard around the neck when he scoops him up.

"I think he approves," Ryan beams at Shenna who is still feeling shell-shocked from it all.

Putting his free arm around Shenna, Ryan pulls her into a group hug.

Later that morning, Ryan takes Neirin to the dig while Shenna gives a home tutoring lesson. How she manages to concentrate is beyond her, but she supposes her training, and natural instinct to do whatever she is doing to the best of her ability, wins through.

On her own in the quiet cottage, Shenna sits on the settee and looks across at a photo-frame standing next to the television. She is happy and laughing in the photo and Cade is right there at her side, his smile as boyishly enchanting as ever. It had been one of the main attractions for her – she'd loved his ability to smile no matter what.

What's the use of being miserable, he'd say with a huge grin, life goes on and whatever is troubling you today won't matter half as much tomorrow.

Moving over to the photo Shenna picks it up and touches Cade's face through the glass.

"Am I doing the right thing, Cade? Or am I just being a coward...a weak excuse of a woman who can't stand up for herself and her child?"

"You're not weak," Ryan states having let himself in with the key she had given him that morning, "and you're no coward."

Shenna almost drops the photo as she spins towards Ryan with a hand held over her frantically beating heart. Then, realising what she is holding, Shenna turns to replace the photo next to the television.

"I didn't expect you," she states the obvious while catching her breath. "Where's Neirin, is he with you?"

"No, he's helping Sadie and Roz clean up some new finds – I came to make sure you weren't brooding over your decision to marry me," he tells her and manages to close the gap between them without her realising. Putting a finger under her chin he gently tips her face up to look at him. "I'm going to make you and Neirin very happy – I know we can make this work."

Before Shenna can pull away Ryan's lips are on hers and the heat they had felt that morning springs just as quickly into life.

Just how deep can a kiss be – Shenna finds herself held tight against Ryan's taught body and still doesn't feel close enough! The fingers of one hand are twined in his hair the other gliding over the muscles in his back. Too many clothes...to many barriers...I need to feel you...want to feel your hands on me...need to...need to...

Gathering her up, Ryan holds her to his chest and strides over to the stairs then hesitates briefly. "I want you, Shenna," and his flaming eyes pierce her with need. At her brief nod he climbs the stairs to her bedroom then lets her slide down his body to stand in front of him.

There are net curtains up at the window so they are hidden from prying eyes. "Curtains open or closed?" he asks with a patience that amazes him.

Looking at his broad chest Shenna knows she wants to see him naked. "Open," she decides and quivers with anticipation.

With deft hands they take enormous pleasure in removing each other's clothes. Their hands caress each portion of flesh as they reveal it, their lips tasting and their teeth nibbling as if feasting slowly on a long awaited mouth-watering dish.

Her body is toned but womanly, and Ryan kisses the silver lines on her lower abdomen in appreciation of that fact.

When his hot mouth moves lower Shenna can

barely stand. Her fingers clench tighter in his hair pulling him to her wantonly. When his tongue finds her moisture and heat she cries out with the pleasure that burst through her then almost collapses onto the bed.

Ryan guides her descent and follows her onto the soft, cool quilt. His mouth has returned to hers now, and she can taste her saltiness on his lips – an erotic flavour that Shenna had long forgotten.

But Ryan is giving her new memories to savour, and when he pushes into her he does so gently and waits for her body to adjust.

"Did I hurt you," he asks looking down into her smouldering green eyes."

Shenna smiles up at him and raises her hips in answer then feels him push deeper in response.

He takes her slowly, watching her passion build...feeling it tighten her body until she bows beneath him and cries out with an orgasm that almost pulls him over the edge with her. But Ryan somehow manages to hold himself back and now he is pounding into her, taking Shenna right back up and flying with her. "Together...!"

They had cried that one word in unison and took the leap into heaven at full tilt.

There was no going back now – they both knew it and clung to each other like survivors of a ship-wreck who had found each other in a vast ocean of happenstance. They would save each other – would give each other what was missing in their lives. And love...well...love was overrated and they would manage on the respect and friendship that had grown strong between them.

"Is it true?" Gail asks as the three of them sit at their usual pool side table to watch their children have their swim lesson. "You know what I mean," Gail frowns at Shenna as she plays the innocent, "you heard Neirin talking to Tommy and the twins about his new 'daddy' just as well as I did!"

Juliette arrives at the table, coffee in hand, just in time to hear Gail's rant. "Well I didn't – what have I missed and what new daddy are we talking about?"

Taking a sip of her tea, Shenna remains tight-lipped.

"I heard Neirin telling Tommy and the twins about having a new daddy," she raises her eyebrows at Juliette, "but Shenna won't spill the beans – I think it has to be Ryan Tempest...who else has little miss isolation had time or opportunity to meet?"

Turning to Shenna, Juliette sees the pink in her

cheeks and smiles with delight. "It's true...it's written all over you – when did this happen?"

Knowing that they won't let it go, Shenna decides to enjoy the moment. "Ryan asked me a couple of days ago and I said yes – Neirin is over the moon, he really loves Ryan."

"And you..?" Gail probes quietly.

Hesitating to put a label on her feelings for Ryan, Shenna just shrugs and says, "We're good together, I think we can make each other very happy."

She sees the look of concern pass between her friends but doesn't acknowledge it. What Ryan has proposed makes perfect sense for them; they like and respect each other and are certainly compatible in bed, the rest will develop in time, or not. As long as they like and respect each other they will have as much if not more than most couples do after a few years of marriage.

At the end of the lesson, they collect their children and get ready to go home. "Is Tommy coming over for a play-date?" Shenna asks Gail as they make their way out to the car park.

"Are you sure he won't be in the way?" Gail asks politely.

"Was Neirin in the way when he went home with

you last week?" Shenna asks dryly. "Nothing is going to change – in fact," Shenna turns to Juliette, "if you wouldn't mind bringing the twins over I'd love to have them all for the day – we can show them the pottery you've found on the dig site," she smiles at Neirin.

He nods and grins enthusiastically.

"Well, if you're sure I'll follow behind you," and the women take care of securing the children into their car seats.

After snapping Tommy's car seat into Shenna's car, Gail straps her son in and gives him a kiss along with a warning to behave. Then she turns to Shenna with a 'have you lost your mind' look.

"Call me if it gets too much," Gail smiles doubtfully, "I'm not going anywhere or doing anything that can't be interrupted so don't be a martyr, ok?"

As Shenna drives home the boys in the back are chatting and giggling and she can't help smiling at her own gluttony for punishment. On their best behaviour the four boys can be a joy, but if something sparks them off, especially one of the twins, they can go from best friends to mortal enemies in a heartbeat.

"I've warned them to behave," Juliette tells her as

Shenna steps out of her car. "And I've told them that you won't hesitate to call me if they don't," turning mum's evil eye on her boys Juliette pauses dramatically, "then their father will come and fetch them which will put him in an awful mood and guess who will pay for that?"

Knowing that keeping a firm hand on the boys is the only way Juliette can keep any semblance of order, Shenna stands back silently and watches.

But when Juliette drives away she watches, a little apprehensively, as the boys turn their heads to look at each other and grin like the mischievous brothers they are. Help!

"Ok, who fancies going to the archaeology dig site?" she asks and the four boys all agree with a loud shout of 'ME'. "Ok, well, there are a couple of rules that we need to get straight," and the twins immediately grimace at each other. "The dig site is not a playground, it can be dangerous," and she pauses to look at each child in turn, "but it can also be great fun. Neirin will be able to show you the pottery that he has helped to dig up and tell you what he's learned about the people who would have used it. Then there is the display of items actually found in this area by local people who had been walking in the forest or by visitors to the area – you'll be able to read their names next to the items and see if you recognise anyone."

The boys were all nodding enthusiastically and Shenna leads the way over to the visitor's centre where they are greeted by Sadie and Roz.

"Hey, Neirin," Sadie smiles at her little helper, "did you bring some friends to help with the dig?"

Neirin blushes and laughs, "No, these are my friends and we've come to see the displays you made and I can show them what we dug up."

"Give me a minute and I'll get the keys," Roz tells them all and turns to go over to Ryan's office. The man himself follows her out and both of them make their way over to the waiting group.

"Got yourself a handful I see," and Ryan smiles down at the group of boys who are looking way up at him with awestruck expressions. "I think your new addition to our visitor's centre is going to come in handy again," he tells Roz.

Turning to Shenna, Roz explains, "We had a group of school children in this morning – about ten or so – and I got some paper and crayons out for them to draw whatever objects they found interesting." Ryan opens the port-a-cabin door and the children file in followed by the adults.

A collective 'wow' is breathed out by all four boys; even Neirin is impressed with the changes that have been made.

"I made room for a few small tables and chairs down that end of the display," she points to her right, "and moved all of the actual display items up this end. That way we have an area that is child friendly where they won't be getting told off all the time for touching things."

"This is great, Roz," Shenna smiles, "and just right for keeping little hands and minds busy."

"And this is the start of our wall of fame," Roz states mysteriously to the boys. "Each member of a visiting group gets to draw whichever object they chose and the members of the dig team pick out a winner."

All the boys look eager but Tommy gets really excited. "What do we win?" he asks with large round eyes.

Pointing to the wall, Roz shows them this morning's wining drawing with the name and age of the child that drew it underneath. "If your drawing makes it to the wall of fame everyone who visits this display will get to see your work, plus..." and again she pauses to look from one eager little face to another, "...I have a small treat for the winner."

Ryan looks to Sadie and Roz and asks, "Would you mind if I steal Shenna away for a few minutes – I need to update her about the changes around here?"

Sadie looks at the floor and shakes her head but Roz just says, "We'll be fine, don't rush on our account."

Looking at the dig site Shenna can see that it is making some real headway. "What are these small trenches all about?" she asks as they pass by.

"We believe it's the outline of a house emerging, probably lived in by the family that used the pot Neirin has been uncovering," Ryan tells her before stepping up into his office.

Going over to the coffee pot, Ryan begins getting out mugs and looking busy.

"What's wrong?" Shenna waits for him to turn then asks the same question again. "What's wrong, Ryan is it to do with the changes you wanted to talk to me about?"

He nods and places a mug of coffee in front of her. "Felicity has gone – I ordered her off the site just after the school party left this morning!"

"You...she...why?" Shenna is virtually speechless

at this unexpected turn of events.

"Felicity heard Sadie and Roz talking about us getting married and, according to the girls, she lost it big time." He takes a sip of his coffee and contemplates the black liquid through troubled blue eyes. "When I came out of my office to see what was going on she lunged at me with murder in her eyes – I swear, I've never seen her so out of control," he looks over at Shenna and wonders what she is thinking.

"She said you were an item," Shenna spoke softly not sure where her thoughts were taking her, "that you and she were lovers but she also said that she didn't want children...and that you did..." Her voice trails off as an awful thought dawns on her.

He sees it in her eyes the moment the idea enters her head. "No, I am not marrying you just to get myself a readymade family," he states firmly. "I care for both of you and I'll do my best to see you both safe and happy." Watching her nod automatically Ryan can still see the doubts. "We're neither of us young and fanciful - what we can give each other is real and grounded and will work if we're both committed to it."

Moving round the desk Ryan drops to his

haunches to look directly into Shenna's worried eyes. "I learned at my mother's knee what a flimsy emotion love is but I care for you Shenna, and Neirin too, and I believe we can give him the parents he deserves."

Nodding, Shenna covers Ryan's hands with her own, "Yes, I believe we can."

With relief washing over him Ryan pulls Shenna to her feet and holds her to him. A moment of hesitation passes then he feels her arms encircle his waist and knows the storm has passed.

"I will take care of you both," he whispers and kisses the top of her head with reverent tenderness.

Shenna answers without the need for words – her arms tighten about him and her cheek nuzzles into his chest. She feels safe here and she wants Neirin to feel safe too.

I know some people would think I'm crazy but I have to trust my instincts. Ryan cares deeply for Neirin and would never hurt us, I think that's about all I'm entitled to ask for in return for what he is offering.

"Where is Felicity now?" Shenna asks, as they reluctantly pull apart.

"I made her pack all her things then drove her to

the airport – she's on her way to Heathrow then Africa so you won't be bumping into her any time soon," Ryan assures her.

Letting out a sigh of relief Shenna smiles up at him, "That's kind of good to know," she tells him, "but I am sorry that things turned so ugly – I know you must have cared about her once."

"I did, but it was never enough – Felicity wanted marriage, believed herself in love with me for years though she had many lovers besides me in that time."

Stepping back, Shenna stares up at him in amazement. "She did...why?"

Looking at her dumbfounded expression Ryan doesn't try to pretend he doesn't understand the question and is even gratified that she thinks highly enough of him to ask it. "Felicity likes to own things, she's a collector and I think that's what drew her to archaeology in the first place," he muses. "But she doesn't stop at possessions, objects, no...Felicity collects men like trophy's...she..."

Neirin came to the port-a-cabin door with a drawing in his hands and a broad smile across his face.

Turning to Shenna, Ryan lowers his voice, "Let's

not talk about her anymore, Felicity's gone and we can get back to being happy again."

Happy? Yes, they had been happy once the strangeness of the situation had eased. "Your right," she tells him and reaches up to place a kiss on his surprised lips.

A giggle from the doorway makes Shenna blush. "Are you laughing at me, young man," and she reaches out to tickle her delighted son while Ryan looks on, glad that they will soon be a family.

CHAPTER EIGHT

The dead dog is laid on the doorstep with a kitchen knife sticking out of its chest and a note stuffed into its gaping mouth.

Shenna can't help herself, she almost steps on the dog as she makes to leave the cottage and her scream is probably heard from a couple of miles away.

She doesn't see Ryan, closely followed by Carl and Paul, race through the trees from the dig site to find out what is wrong. The moment he sees the dog Ryan doesn't need any explanation.

"Take it back to the dig," Ryan tells the two men, "I'll bury it later." But just as Ryan steps to Shenna's side to usher her inside, Paul calls him back.

"Ryan, I think you ought to look at this!"

He had removed a ball of paper from the dogs open mouth and smoothed it out enough to read the message on it.

Shenna stands trembling in the doorway her eyes alighting on the paper that Ryan now holds. "What is it – what does it say?"

But Ryan doesn't answer; he just folds the paper and slips it into his pocket giving Paul a warning look before turning back to Shenna.

"It's the same as all the rest," he tells her angrily, though his arms about her shoulders couldn't have been more gentle and reassuring. "If I ever get my hands on this maniac I'll teach him a lesson in pain that he won't soon forget!"

Guiding Shenna to sit on the settee, Ryan sits beside her and just holds her until the trembling stops. "I think Neirin should stay with your family for a while," he suggests and feels Shenna stiffen and pull away.

"You think he's in danger...?" Her eyes are wide with shock and her face has lost all colour. "What exactly did that note say – I want to read it," she demands and holds a none too steady hand out towards him.

Heaving a heavy sigh of regret, Ryan pulls the

note from his pocket and hands it to her.

A sharp intake of breath is covered by a hand that is now shaking with fear. "This isn't like the others..." she looks up from the note with terror in her eyes, "...this is a threat on Neirin's life...but why...I don't understand...?"

"Some sick bastard is getting off on the terror he knows he's inflicting on you." Ryan stands to pace the sitting room in frustration. "And he must have been watching for me to leave before leaving that damned dog on the doorstep for you or Neirin to find!" Then Ryan stops suddenly and looks at Shenna. "Or maybe not..." he frowns and walks back to sit by her side on the settee.

"What are you thinking?" she asks when he sits chewing over his thoughts in silence.

"I'm thinking that it might not be a coincidence that Neirin is having a sleepover at Tommy's," Ryan speculates softly. "Think about it, the last animal that was left in such an obvious, in your face place, was the squirrel hung by its neck with a make-shift noose to frighten you when you opened your front door – Neirin was having a sleepover with Tommy that time too!"

"I don't get it...what about all the other animals,

they were just as horrible to find even if they weren't on the doorstep," she shudders and Ryan puts an arm round her shoulders and pulls her to him.

"I think they were red herrings," and nods to confirm his own thoughts. "We've been thinking that it was Neirin who was meant to find the animals, starting with the badger being left where he would certainly have come across it had he gone out to collect the chicken eggs as he often does."

"But now you don't think so...?" It's all as clear as mud to Shenna, but she can see that Ryan is convinced.

"He's been threatening Neirin to frighten you – this whole thing has been about inflicting as much fear on you as possible and the one way of ensuring he did that was by threatening Neirin's safety."

"Well, he succeeded!" Shenna shifts nearer to Ryan feeling his strength surrounding her. "I've never been so terrified in my entire life!"

Later that morning Shenna calls Gail and asks to come round for a chat before she brings Neirin back home.

"I know it's a lot to ask," she tells Gail, "but I don't have anyone else, my parents died years ago and I don't have any siblings."

"Will you stop!" Gail puts a fresh mug of strong tea in front of Shenna then sits to drink her own. "It isn't a problem – Tommy will love it and Terry won't mind in the least – he loves kids."

"I'm going to call into the police station on the way to pick up some things for Neirin – I think this has gone beyond the possibility of a kids prank."

"Good lord!" Gail is totally shocked. "I assumed you'd done that already!"

"It isn't that I haven't thought about it," Shenna smiles ruefully, "I just didn't want to bring the law down on some poor kids head if it was just a prank. Once a child gets a police record it follows them for a very long time."

Putting a hand to her forehead, Gail closes her eyes and tries to draw on her innate patience. "From what you've said this has been going on for weeks – do you know any kids that would sustain this kind of activity over so long?"

"No," Shenna concedes, "but I did when I was in school. There was an older boy who loved torturing animals – he used to show some of the other kids how he did it in the playground. It was really ugly and cruel, and that's why he was expelled."

"Ok. Ok. I know some boys go through that sort

of phase," Gail concedes reluctantly, "and some of them grow up to be serial killers. Shenna...I'll gladly keep Neirin with us for as long as it takes to catch this butcher, but you need to be extremely careful...this doesn't sound like a kid to me!"

Nodding, Shenna agrees. "Ryan has moved in to dispel the vulnerable widow idea that this creep might be clinging to – but the dog incident happened after he had left for the dig." Shenna considers then looks horrified over at Gail, "I don't know why I didn't think of it before...he must have been watching for Ryan to leave...actually watching my house!" Wide eyed and amazed at her own stupidity, Shenna follows that thought, "He could still have been there...don't they like to see the results...the terror...isn't that what they get off on?"

"Where are you going?" Gail asks with concern when Shenna abruptly pushes back her chair and pulls her coat on. "Don't do anything without Ryan – Shenna..." Gail actually swings her friend round to face her, "don't even think of going after this man without taking Ryan with you...and stay out of the forest – if he is out there he'd just love to get you alone...you don't know what the hell might happen then!"

"Stop worrying – just take care of Neirin for me, I'll be back later with clothes and things for him." With that Shenna races out of Gail's house and drives back to the cottage, completely forgetting to call into the police station as she had planned.

Ryan is just closing the front door of the cottage when Shenna arrives home and pulls the car to an abrupt stop. He moves over to her as she steps out of the car and slams the door behind her.

"You knew!" she accuses and pushes a finger hard into Ryan's chest. "Damn it, Ryan!"

"Not being a mind reader I have no idea what you're talking about." But he could take a good guess.

"Don't give me that!" she rages, blinded by fear. "You knew we were being watched, that this wasn't someone leaving things at random, at night when no one would be about. This morning was different...they waited for you to leave and that means they were here this morning, watching, waiting for me to be alone..." Her hand flies up to cover her mouth, a scream is bubbling up to escape but she won't give the slimy creep any more exhibitions of fear.

Ryan took her in his arms and held her, just held

her tight and safe. "I won't let him get to you, Shenna - from now on we stick together!"

"I'm worried about Neirin," she tells him, "I've asked Gail to keep him with her until this is over - but if I'm not with him I can't protect him!" How do I just hand that responsibility over - a sleepover is one thing but living there and for who knows how long...

"That's understandable," Ryan doesn't try to dismiss or smooth over her worries, "I'll miss having him around and worry about him too - but it's the right thing to do, Shenna. I don't know why, but this man is fixated on you and Neirin is safer away from here."

"Away from me you mean," and Ryan feels the sob she tries to stifle against his chest. I'll kill the bastard if I ever get my hands on him!

"He's a coward, Shenna...probably someone who started out by having a crush on you and then began stalking you - I don't believe it's ever been about Neirin," but that doesn't make Ryan feel any better and he rubs his large gentle hand up and down her back.

"He could be watching us right now," Shenna mumbles then raises her head to look up at Ryan. "Couldn't we look - go into the forest now and see if we can find where he's been watching from – we might even find a few clues as to who he is?"

Shifting his feet, Ryan has to confess. "We did that already," he tells her warily, "Paul and I searched the surrounding area but found nothing...not a bloody thing!"

Instead of getting angry as Ryan expects, Shenna blows out a breath and rubs her hands over her tired face.

"I can't take this, Ryan," and looks up to see him watching her intently, "maybe I should do what they want and leave – at least then I'd have Neirin with me."

"So you just walk away," Ryan's face and voice have hardened, "pack up and say nice knowing you but I don't need you anymore – is that it, Shenna?"

Shocked by the hurt she has caused, Shenna reaches out to touch his cheek. "No, Ryan, that's not it at all...I wasn't talking about walking away from you...I just...damn it, Ryan...I have no idea what to do for the best!"

Again he wraps her in his arms and swears he'll get to the bottom of this somehow. The thought of losing Shenna, and Neirin, is more painful that he could have imagined – they were his now, he realises.

Later that day Shenna rings round the parents of her home tutoring group and tells them that she has to cancel lessons for a week or two but will continue as soon as possible. The excuse she gives is a family crisis. Well if this isn't a family crisis I don't know what is!

From that moment on Shenna is never out of Ryan's sight. She goes with him to the dig and even learns how to scrape at the soil so as not to damage anything that might be beneath it. She finds herself thinking of the hours Neirin has spent doing this, the joy he found in finding even the smallest piece of pottery. I know you'll miss this Neirin, but I have to keep you safe...and there will be other digs...other times you can enjoy sharing with Ryan. Shenna looks up to see the man himself watching her from his office doorway and waves a hand. He loves you Neirin, whether Ryan believes in love or not, I can see it in the way he teaches you, the patience and the care...

"You look lost in thought," Ryan tells her when he walks to Shenna's side. "I spoke to Gail a moment ago and Neirin is fine – asking some awkward questions, but that was to be expected," he tells Shenna as she stands. "Want to go over and see him later?"

Giving him a smile that doesn't quite reach her eyes, Shenna nods grateful that he understands. "I feel empty without him," she explains, "Neirin is who I am...has been since the day he came kicking and screaming into my life. I love him so much."

Yes, Ryan can see that, yet it doesn't sit well with him. Not that he doesn't want her to love her son...but Ryan's experiences with his own mother have twisted his views on love...he is learning a lot from Shenna and Neirin...he just isn't sure he has the same capacity for emotion that he knows Shenna does.

"You want to go now?" Ryan's heart does a flip at the beaming smile that suddenly lights her face. Wow!

"Oh please – I know you have a lot to do...but..." her arms suddenly fly up to wrap around his neck and Ryan has to steady them both. "Thank you," she whispers next to Ryan's ear and causes a shock of pleasure to shoot down his spine. "I'll get cleaned up in five minutes flat, you see." And before he can stop her, Shenna heads for her cottage.

Hearing a giggle, Ryan turns to see Sadie and Roz grinning like loons, even Carl and Paul are looking at him with soppy smiles.

"What?!" He stares from one to the other but none of the smiles disappear. I must be losing my touch!

"It's just nice," Sadie dares to say and keeps right on grinning when he scowls at her.

Giving up on being the scary boss, which obviously isn't working anyway, Ryan returns the smile and gives Sadie a wink. "I won't be gone long – just stay in sight of the camp and each other – ok?"

All four heads bob in unison and Ryan heads for the cottage. Shenna has only been gone a couple of minutes but suddenly he picks up the pace and curses himself for a fool.

For christ's sake...you let her go off on her own! You can't afford to let your guard down like that...what if she's not there...what if he's...

"Ok, I'm ready and I'm sure it didn't take me five minutes," Shenna laughs as she locks her front door then stops dead when she turns to see Ryan's desperately worried face. "What's happened...is it Neirin...has somethi-"

He was kissing her with all the fear pouring out of him. Hell's teeth, what an idiot...what if she had been taken...what if...

"What is it?" Shenna asks gently, her palm lying soft against his pale cheek.

Shaking his head Ryan pulls her back into his arms. "I left you alone...I let my guard down and you could have been hurt...or..."

Her arms snake around his waist and her head lays against his chest listening to the heavy beat of his heart. "I'm fine, and you can't be with me every minute of every day – you have to trust me to look after myself."

Never! I won't let you out of my sight again! Idiot!

"Ok, let's go see Neirin," Ryan suggests and keeps his arm about her shoulders as they walk to Shenna's car. His insides are still shaking and for once he's glad he doesn't have to drive.

When they reach Gail's she tells them that Neirin appears to be pining a bit. He often sits by himself, reading or drawing, but he doesn't seem to get very far with either.

"He's missing you – I think this is just what he needs," Gail smiles.

When they go through to the lounge Terry calls "hi" then continues to watch the football match on TV.

Neirin is sitting on the stairs with a book staring into space. When he hears Terry's greeting he turns to see who it is.

"Mum, Ryan," he calls out and runs to them not sure which to go to first.

Ryan scoops him up and they enfold each other in a group hug.

"Have you come to take me home...am I going to work on the dig again," Neirin asks barely taking a breath.

Not wanting to interfere, Ryan stays quiet and waits to follow Shenna's lead.

"Not today, Neirin," Shenna strokes the boys hair and kisses his cheek. "We want to, but I have to be away a lot at the moment and I can't leave you on your own."

"I could stay with Ryan," Neirin's pleading eyes turn on the man at his mum's side, but he can see the answer already.

"I'd love that, Neirin, but I have a lot of work to do – the dig is getting really busy," he tells him and ruffles Neirin's hair gently.

"We miss you too," Shenna tells him and wraps him in a hug, never wanting to let him go.

With his bottom lip trembling, Neirin tries to do as his dad has told him and be the man of the house. "I'm ok mum, I know you're busy." And he includes Ryan in the look he gives her. "Can I...I mean, may I read my book now?"

Setting him back on his feet, Shenna crouches to eyelevel with Neirin. "I love you more than anything in the world...you remember that," she tells him and just manages to kiss his cheek again before he returns to sit on the stairs holding his book.

On the drive back both Shenna and Ryan are quiet and broody. Not until they reach the cottage does either one of them speak.

"That was awful," Ryan tells her, his hands rubbing over tired eyes. "I don't know how my mother did it."

Shenna knows that he is referring to the many times he'd been left alone as a child and her heart breaks for that child.

"Maybe she had no choice...or didn't think she had."

"And maybe she just didn't care," he sighs. He doesn't feel sorry for himself; Ryan has built a lucrative career out of an interest that one of her johns had told him about. He had been one of the nicer men his mum had brought home. "I don't remember having anything like what you and Neirin have so it's all a bit of a mystery to me – but that doesn't mean I don't care," he tells her and turns to see Shenna wiping away a tear.

"I'm sorry...I just can't imagine leaving Neirin like that...he'd be terrified."

Yeah, so was I...and hungry...and cold and filthy to boot!

"I shouldn't have brought that up, I'm sorry." Pushing out of the car Ryan strides around it to reach Shenna's door and open it for her. "I haven't thought about my mother in years, I don't know what possessed me to think about her now!"

Shenna allows Ryan to help her out of the car and locks it behind her. When they step inside the cottage it feels cold and more unwelcoming than Shenna has ever known it before.

Holding her hand out to Ryan she waits for him to take it then tells him, "Take me to bed, Ryan...I want to feel safe and warm – right now...I feel empty and cold."

"Come then," he smiles and walks beside her up the staircase, "we'll warm each other up and stay safe in bed."

Losing all sense of self, Shenna moves against Ryan with so much need inside her and wanting to be filled by him. His touch trails over her, into her and sends her mind away from all the worry and hurt.

Moving down his body, kissing the strength of his muscles bunched in his stomach, Shenna finds him hard and waiting for her.

Her mouth isn't gentle. Taking him in, Shenna tastes and nips and pleasures him until Ryan reaches down to ease her back up the bed.

But after kissing him with the same hunger, Shenna sits astride Ryan and takes the length of him deep inside her. A cry escapes her and Shenna's head falls back, when she rides him it is hard and fast and Ryan can only go with her.

The familiar tightening works up her body and down to her groins and the heat that burns between them.

Her cry of release is matched by Ryan's roar and they collapse into each other's arms and hold on tight.

The explosion could be heard for miles. Ryan shoots naked out of bed and rapidly pulls on a pair of jeans. Going to the window he can see the visitor's port-a-cabin going up in flames.

Shenna is less quick to come around but shrugs on a pair of jeans and a jumper without troubling for underwear. Looking out of the window she can see Ryan running through the forest and can hear him call the names of his crew. One by one they appear in the clearing, she can't make them out fully, but she can count five people including Ryan.

"Is everyone safe...are you all ok?" Ryan looks frantically from one crew member to the next, until he can be sure they are not harmed. Then he walks to one side to get a better view of the burning port-a-cabin, "Any ideas as to what happened?" he asks having to shout above the loud cracks and mini explosions.

Everyone looks at everyone else, all of them shaking their heads in confusion. "Has there been anyone hanging around, someone taking an interest in the dig?"

Again they all shake their heads and Ryan gives up. Taking out his mobile phone Ryan calls the police and fire brigade then ushers everyone up to the cottage.

"Just take a seat, we'll arrange somewhere for you all to sleep," Ryan tells them as he makes his way towards the kitchen. "It wouldn't be safe for you down there, even if they manage to put the fire out without the other port-a-cabins being damaged."

Filling the kettle he puts it on to boil then returns to the sitting room. He can see both girls shivering, probably with shock and tells them he'll get them a blanket.

Taking the stairs two at a time, Ryan shouts up to Shenna. "Do you have any spare blankets – I think the girls are in shock they're both shivering down there."

Entering the bedroom, Ryan finds it empty and immediately goes to Neirin's room. When he finds that empty too his mind begins to whirl and he has to hold on to the door-frame to keep from falling.

Grabbing the quilt from Neirin's bed he heads back downstairs and hands it to the girls. To the young men he gives a signal with his head that he wants to talk to them outside.

"Shenna's not upstairs," Ryan tells them and is amazed that his voice is steady. "We're going round the back of the house to see if she's in the back yard – be careful, this fucker managed to get the drop on me before, just keep your eyes wide open."

The three men stride stealthily to the back of the house, each one looking into shadows and listening for tell-tale signs.

Nothing! The rear garden was empty with no signs that anyone has been there. The chickens give a disturbed squawk but that is it.

They hear the sound of sirens, the police and fire brigade have arrived. "Carl, you're fastest on your feet, go and tell the police I need one of them up here right now!"

"Paul, I want you to stay with the girls – keep them safe – I'm just going to take a quick look around."

They all move off, it's dark, but when they reach the front of the cottage the sky is lit up by the fire and there are people busy trying to put it out.

Ryan stands looking through the trees – it had been a diversion and the bastard who set it up had planned it well.

CHAPTER NINE

She was freezing and Shenna's head was throbbing painfully. She tried to move but she was trussed up good and tight. The bumps in the road cause her head to bash painfully against a metal floor. A van perhaps, or a lorry.

Losing consciousness, Shenna doesn't feel the van pull over and stop. When a hypodermic needle plunges into her arm she gives only a small whine of pain then is fully out for the count.

Coming to again, Shenna can feel a cold floor beneath her body, concrete or quarry tiles maybe. Her head won't clear – Shenna can hear voices. Ryan! But she fades out again and the nightmares begin.

One minute she is standing at her bedroom

window watching Ryan running through the trees calling out to his crew, the next she feels a pain at the back of her head and the world goes dark. But before she blanks out completely she hears a man's voice.

"You're mine now; I can take all the time I want!"

Shivering herself awake, Shenna can't make out anything, but realises her captive has put a hood over her head.

Oh please don't let it end like this, Neirin will be distraught.

The thought of her son makes Shenna determined to survive, she'll do whatever the pervert wants and wait for a chance to escape.

Yes, I can do that – I'll just let my mind go to another place and not struggle or protest...I won't upset him in any way that might spark him to violence!

She waits...and waits. The silence is deafening, the cold biting into her flesh and the ropes burning into her wrists and ankles when she tries to work them loose.

Why isn't he doing something...he must have taken me for a reason. Her mind starts to go into overdrive. What if he just leaves me here – maybe he really did just want me to leave, but why?

Her teeth are chattering and her bladder involuntarily opens. The heat of her urine brings a welcome moment of warmth but is soon replaced by an even more intense cold.

Shenna is almost glad when the dark claims her again, though her dreams are not much better than the nightmare she is living.

Ryan is holding Neirin's hand, helping him to place a rose on his mother's coffin. "No...Neirin...I'm here," she mumbles against the gag tied around her mouth, her head thrashing wildly.

"Don't worry, Neirin you'll live with me now," and she watches Ryan bend down and scoop her little man up into his arms. "We'll look after each other and I'll be your dad now."

When she comes to again, Shenna's face is wet with tears.

Oh please help me...someone help me.

"You awake?" A boot strikes hard at her side and makes Shenna cry out. "I got your boy in the next room – god that was easy, you just think about what I'm doing to him while you're lying out here. He'll be pissed when he knows you're in the next room and doing nothing to help him!"

Screaming against the gag, Shenna tries to plead

with her captor, but all she gets for her trouble is a kick in the head that almost knocks her unconscious again.

Don't black out! Don't black out! Think! Think! Think!

Ryan comes back to the cottage to find a police constable waiting to talk to him. "I understand you're in charge of the site where a port-a-cabin has been set alight," the constable has to move quickly to keep up with Ryan as he strides past him and into the cottage.

"I don't give a flying fuck about any port-a-cabin," Ryan shouts as he turns on the uniformed man, "a woman has been kidnapped and her son may be in imminent danger!"

"What!"

Then Ryan turns angry eyes on Carl. "I tried to tell him..."

"What's all this about – whose been kidnapped and where is the son you think is in danger?"

"The woman is Shenna Williams, this is her cottage," Ryan swings his arm out and around, "her son, Neirin, is staying with friends in the town...we were afraid for his safety and thought it best if he were away from here for a time."

"Give me the address and name of the people this

boy is staying with," the constable takes out his radio and repeats the name and address that Ryan gives him. "That's right," the officer tells the radio controller, "Shenna Williams is missing and her son is believed to be in imminent danger, I want a police car to check that the boy is safe."

That done the officer turns to the other occupants of the room. "I want names and statements from each of you, anything you may have seen or heard no matter how insignificant you think it might be."

Ryan is pacing, almost pulling his hair out in frustration. I should be out there searching, she could be anywhere by now – or lying injured in the woods.

"I'll start with you if I may," the officer tells Ryan. "Better to get it down in writing while the memories are still fresh."

They go into the kitchen and sit at the breakfast table. "Now sir, when did all this start?"

Ryan tells him about the butchered animals and the notes pinned to them telling Shenna to leave. But when he starts telling him about the dog and the note threatening Neirin's life, Ryan has to take a couple of breaths to steady himself. "It was bad, gruesome, and it frightened Shenna half to death," Ryan pushes both hands back through his longer than usual blond hair.

"That's when we decided to ask Gail and her husband to keep Neirin with them for a while, just to keep him safe while we sorted this mess out."

"And you didn't at any time think to contact the police?" The officer looks staggered by the thought.

"We thought about it, but Shenna believed it was kids acting out, just teenagers going through a gruesome phase." Shaking his head, even Ryan can't believe he went along with Shenna on that. "She was supposed to call into the police station on the way home from dropping Neirin off at Gail's, but she got sidetracked and I just wanted to keep her in my sight at all times."

The officer nods and continues to write in his notepad.

"It was just a few dead animals," Ryan snaps angrily, "can you honestly tell me that the police would have been bothered to investigate a few dead animals!"

Pulling on his training, the officer doesn't respond to Ryan's outburst but waits for him to calm down.

"I can see how you might think that," the officer tells Ryan quietly, "but it isn't just a few dead animals now, is it sir?"

Putting his head in his hands, Ryan stares down at the table and tries to think.

"All I'm saying is, if we had known earlier we could have at least looked into the notes – there could have been fingerprints or..."

"There wasn't!" Ryan lifts his head to stare straight into the officer's eyes. "I sent them to a friend of mine; he put them through rigorous forensic testing and got nothing." Getting to his feet, Ryan decides the time for talking has come to an end. "I'm going now, and taking Carl and Paul with me," the officer makes to protest but Ryan cuts him off. "It's been almost an hour now since Shenna went missing – I'm going out in to that forest to see if we can find her, damn it!"

The officer doesn't try to stop him, and doesn't think he could if he did try. "I'll continue taking statements from the ladies; as you heard...a detective is on his way and will no doubt bring other officers with him – I'll send them out to help as soon as they get here!"

With a nod to the officer Ryan turns to Carl and Paul. "Are you up for helping me search?"

Without hesitation the two get to their feet and follow Ryan outside. The night is still dark and very cold, but none of them seem to notice.

When Shenna next awakes she is groggy and can't keep her thoughts in order. Drugged. I think I've been drugged.

She hears a movement close by but doesn't think whatever made it is in the same room. Then she hears a terrible scream...a child's scream... Neirin! "Nnooo!" Her scream goes on and on in her head and the child continues to scream too. "Oh God, please help him...please God help my boy..."

Her world went thankfully silent; her mind sent careening off by the drugs her captor has just injected into her.

"Shenna...Shenna...listen to me Shenna!"

"Cade...?" When Shenna opens her eyes she can see and she is sitting on the fallen tree trunk by the stream...and Cade is by her side.

"You have to listen to me Shenna or you won't survive!"

"You're not real...you can't be."

"I'm as real as you are sitting in our special place in the forest by the stream," he tells her and gives her a familiar lopsided grin.

"Oh Cade...I've missed you so much," and flings her arms around her husband's neck. Drawing back,

Shenna stares up at him. "How can this be...am I dead...are we in heaven?"

Cade's grin slides away and his expression becomes serious. "You're in an old farmhouse down in the cellar, if you don't find a way out you'll die there," he tells her. "You're already becoming ill, the floor is freezing where you're laying and you're clothes are wet – if much more time goes by you'll go hypothermic and fall into unconsciousness then you won't have a chance to save yourself."

Shenna is shaking her head unable to take it all in. "But I'm here with you and I'm not cold at all," and looking around her Shenna smiles at the beauty of the forest in full bloom. "In fact I feel wonderful, never better, and I'm with you...my wonderful husband, I love you so much."

"You have to listen to what I'm telling you, Shenna!" Cade tries to sound firm but Shenna just smiles in delight.

"Come with me," standing, Shenna holds out a hand to Cade, "let's walk by the stream...isn't it lovely, so blue and crystal clear."

Sensing that he is fighting a losing battle, Cade decides to give in then maybe he can talk to her along the way.

The stream ripples over rocks and winds its way round a bend and out of site. "We have a lovely home...I never want to leave here, how lucky we are." Smiling up adoringly at her husband, Shenna has forgotten the other world entirely. Cade knows that the longer she stays the more Shenna will want to stay and the less likely she is to make it back in time to survive.

"We have to talk, Shenna," he tells her softly. "I know you think you can stay here but it isn't your time yet...you have Neirin who needs you more than I do."

Frowning, Shenna looks up at Cade then smiles. "Who's Neirin, I think you've been dreaming."

"No Shenna, it's you who is dreaming, it's the only way I can talk to you, but you have to wake up now...or you never will again!"

Cade walks Shenna to the edge of the stream and tells her to look into the clear water.

"Who's that?" she asks pointing to a still figure, bound and gagged lying on a concrete floor.

"That's you, Shenna and I need to help you get back before it's too late."

"Too late for what...?" Shenna has been enjoying herself, now she begins to feel anxious and afraid.

"Neirin needs you – our son needs you, Shenna. You have to go back and find a way to escape or he'll be all alone in the world. Neirin needs you Shenna."

Neirin needs me. Her thoughts are starting to become clearer and she feels her bindings cut into her flesh as she tries to wriggle free of them. Cade...

When the other officers arrive, Ryan lets out an oath in relief. He signals Carl and Paul to turn around and head back. The officers have dogs and torches; they've been working with mobile phones for light and moving very slowly.

"Ah, you must be Mr Tempest," a detective greets Ryan as he draws level to him. "I'm Detective Brent, the officer who spoke with you earlier has filled me in but I'd like to have a word nevertheless."

"Later!" Ryan snaps and reaches round the detective to take a torch out of the hands of the officer to his rear. "We managed to search the immediate area, but with this," Ryan holds the bright torch in front of him, "we'll make much better time and cover more ground. Paul, Carl, grab a torch each we're going back out." The two young men nod and make to do as he says.

"Mr Tempest!" The detective waits for Ryan to face him. "We will have to talk at some point...about

Mrs Williams and about the fire on your camp site."

Ryan just nods then turns away with Paul and Carl at his side and a bunch of officers up ahead.

The search goes on for the rest of that night, by seven o'clock they've been at it for four hours without a sign of Shenna or her abductor.

"The men are tired," Sergeant Lincoln, head of the search party tells Ryan. "Most of them had already done a full day before volunteering to come out here – we'll take a couple of hours rest then pick up where we left off."

He doesn't want to, but Ryan can see that the men are flagging and he's almost out on his feet himself. But damn it, she's out there...somewhere...what if she's just over the next hill or hidden behind the next bush...

Shenna licks her dry lips then realises that the gag has gone. She is still bound but is now lying on something soft and a lot warmer than the floor had been. But still she shivers. There is nothing covering her and the room is still very cold. But the bone deep ache is easing a little.

"Hello," her voice croaks and Shenna tries again. "Hello."

"Quiet, or I'll put that gag back on!"

"I...I...ok...I j.just wwanted to knnow if yyou were tthere." Her teeth are now chattering so badly that it hurts her jaw trying to clench them shut.

"Stop that racket!"

Something rough was flung over her, it scratches her skin and makes her itch but Shenna is glad of it. "Th.thank yyou."

"Just shut that racket or I'll gut you right now!"

Stay still. Be quiet. Don't make him mad. Stay still. Be quiet. Don't make him mad.

It is a mantra that Shenna repeats over and over – partly to keep from falling into unconsciousness again and partly to help her concentrate her mind.

The drugs are starting to wear off, but Shenna decides not to let on. She lets out an occasional groggy moan but lay as still as a statue.

As still as the woman in the stream...was that a dream...Cade...I talked with Cade...didn't I? But he's dead. Cade's dead. Am I going insane...but it seemed so real...

Sadie and Roz make hot drinks and toast for everyone. They had been to the dig site and rescued their supplies and brought them back to the cottage. There is no way anyone will be staying at the site now.

"It's good of you to do this," Ryan tells them when they bring him a mug of tea and a plate of hot buttered toast. "You've been troopers all along, I'm sorry your first dig is going to be a washout."

"Are you kidding," Sadie tells him askance at the suggestion. "We got to work with the best, and we did make some significant finds."

"Finds which are now blown to hell or burnt beyond recognition," he reminds them.

Moving across the room Sadie picks up a log book and hands it to Ryan. "Even if they are we've fully documented them and we can still learn loads once the mess has been cleared away."

Ryan is amazed. "You still want to continue – after everything that's happened you really want to carry on?"

The girls look at each other and over to Carl and Paul who give them the nod. "Yes we do, and that goes for all of us," Sadie confirms.

Shaking his head in wonder, Ryan leafs through the log book then looks up at his team. "This is excellent work – you've all been exceptional workers and deserve to finish this dig...I'm just not sure I'll be up to heading it when this is all over. I have to find Shenna...and I have Neirin to think about too."

Paul and Carl come to stand by the girls. "We're about ready to head back out, if you want to take another hour no worries – we'll be up on the ridge where we left off earlier."

As tired as his body is, Ryan won't give in. Shenna needs him and he has let her down once by letting the bastard take her – he won't let her down again!

Getting to his feet, Ryan gives the girls a grateful smile then walks out with Paul and Carl at his side.

Shenna is pulled out of her stupor by the sound of a child crying. Neirin! Cade help him...help him...Ryan...

Her thoughts are jumbled, her temperature has risen sharply and Shenna has become seriously ill.

"Cade...? Is that you...?" Her voice is little more than a whispered croak but Cade hears every word.

"I'm with you, Shenna – you need to stay strong – Ryan is nearby."

"Ryan...he loves Neirin..."

"He loves you too, Shenna, as you do him." Cade smiles and strokes her hair. "And that's how it should be – you need to move on and live a full life, I want you to be happy, Shenna...as we were."

"But I love you, Cade..." Her eyes start to close of

their own volition and Cade knows he can't let her fall asleep.

"I know that you will always love me," he tells her and wills her eyes to open and look at him, "as I will always love you and Neirin. But you have a generous heart, Shenna – there's enough love in you to give to Ryan as well."

"I'm so tired...so...so tired..."

A yell goes up in the forest. Ryan's head swivels round in the direction of the yell and makes his leaden legs move faster than he thought possible to find out the latest news.

"Yes sir, I know sir, but the tracks are recent and it isn't an impossible climb for a fit man." The officer on his radio recognises Ryan as he draws near. Frowning, the officer listens to orders being given by Detective Brent then nods and confirms that he has understood. Securing his radio, the officer turns his attention to Ryan. "Mr Tempest, I need you to accompany me to the police station where Detective Brent is waiting to talk to you."

"But I'm needed here!" Ryan protests angrily looking past the officer to a group of other officers huddled over something on the ground. "And what's going on over there – have they found something?"

"Mr Tempest, I am not requesting that you accompany me to the station – if necessary I will read you your rights, place you under arrest and in handcuffs!" He might be young but he knows his job and is determined to carry it out to the best of his ability.

Ryan sees it in his stance and hears it in the tone of the officer's voice - it will be quicker to go with him and get the interview over with than to put up a time wasting struggle.

Feeling herself moving, Shenna's eyes flicker open, but she can't make out where she is. She isn't bound now, but she's too weak to move let alone escape. Cold and barely alive, Shenna moves a hand and realises that she is naked. Naked? Why...naked...Ryan...I'm sorry...s.so...so sorry...

The forest is in full bloom as Shenna walks among the wild flowers on a blissfully warm sunny day. The stream is running faster than she has seen it in a long time, the rushing water tripping over itself in its haste. Listening to the beautiful sound, Shenna walks to sit on a familiar tree trunk lying near the water's edge.

It isn't cold here...I remember feeling so cold...but it's so lovely here...so...

"Shenna...come back, come back Shenna!" Cade is walking beside her as Shenna feels herself moving, lighter than air. "Shenna!"

The forest around her begins to fade, but Shenna wants to stay in the warm sunshine...back there its cold...so cold.

"Cade..." It was no more than a faint croak but Cade fights to keep her with him.

"Shenna, I'm here with you – you stay with me now...you listen to me, Shenna...stay with me. It's Cade – you want to be with me again don't you?"

"Cade...love you Cade..."

"That's right baby, you love me and you want to stay with me so don't fall asleep – ok!

"...ok."

"Five hours! Five goddamned hours wasted going over and over the same questions they asked me before and all because the damned police have to follow procedure!" Ryan strides back and forth, it's late and he's exhausted.

"Carl and Paul are fast away on the beds upstairs," Sadie tells him. "They only came in about an hour ago and just flaked out without even having anything to eat."

Ryan hasn't eaten since the toast Sadie and Roz

gave him that morning, but he couldn't have felt less like food...or sleep.

"I'm going back out." Shrugging on a thick coat and taking up the torch he'd left there that morning, Ryan goes to walk out of the front door.

"But, Ryan..." Roz calls out to detain him, "...you're wiped out and you haven't eaten either."

Ryan lifts a hand of acknowledgement but keeps going out the door. I'm coming Shenna...I'll bring you home tonight for sure!

The weather has taken a turn for the worse. It had been cold last night, but tonight it is bitter...and now it's starting to rain.

By nine o'clock everyone is cold, wet and hungry, and most are tired too – none more so than Ryan.

When the Sergeant calls time on the search, however, Ryan comes right back to life. "No, you can't do this, not again," he protests.

"Mr Tempest...Ryan," the Sergeant can see the pain in his eyes and regrets the necessity to call a halt, "we've done all we can, covered virtually every inch of the forest and there has been no real sign of Mrs Williams."

"So you're giving up – you're just walking away and going home to a nice warm house and a good meal, is that it?"

"Ryan, we're going to go back to the station and follow up on any leads that have come in," the Sergeant tells him, "but I suggest you do exactly that. Go home, get warm and have a hot meal."

The forest is quiet, no one around but Shenna and her captor. The rain has caused the stream to rise and flow more like the river it is part of. Shenna can hear the sound of someone walking into water.

...Cade? ...Ryan?

"Almost there, and now the search has been called off no one will think to look for you right in your own back yard, so to speak."

Cade...Ryan...that voice...

"Welcome home, Shenna...this should do you for the rest of your short life." Heaving and pushing with every ounce of strength they have left, her captor manages to push Shenna's still naked body into a shallow cave in the embankment that will soon be filled by the rising river. "Just do me one favour...die slow!"

There are no more dreams, Shenna can no longer hear Cade's voice calling her back, and the bright sunshine of the forest in full bloom looks more and more attractive and warm.

CHAPTER TEN

Gone, every single one of them! Ryan doesn't know what to do next. He's right, we searched the whole place what else could he do.

It's cold, the rain has stopped but it's still damned cold. Not that Ryan notices – he's been sat in the same place he knows Shenna loves just watching the river roll by.

What the hell! Who is that?!

Standing on the opposite river bank, Ryan can see a man – at least he thinks it's a man.

Christ all bloody mighty...what the hell?!

The man, and it plainly is a man, has daylight shining all around him now and he is signalling to Ryan.

"Who the hell are you...?"

Is he the one...is this the monster who took Shenna!

"Stay where you are...I want to talk to you."

It takes all his control not to dive into the river and swim over to the other side and beat the hell out of him. If he isn't the one who took her then why is he here?

The man starts to walk along the river bank and waves over to Ryan to follow. Not understanding why he should, Ryan hesitates but something about the situation makes him change his mind.

It's dark; at least it was until the stranger showed up. Now Ryan can clearly see to put one foot in front of the other.

I've never seen a light like this – it can't be a torch, it seems be coming from the man himself...which is impossible.

After a couple of minutes the man with the halo of light around his whole body stops and just points across to where Ryan is now standing.

"What? I don't know what you want!"

Then Ryan notices that the man's arm isn't pointing straight at him it's pointing to something lower.

"Down there...?" Ryan points to the river bellow his feet and watches the man nod. "What's down there...what can be so important that you want me to risk my life to get it?"

Then he hears it, a voice so clear and loud in his head.

SHENNA! HURRY!

Jumping into the river, Ryan can only be grateful that it has slowed from earlier. Freezing, he looks back at the man; he is still pointing across the river to where Ryan is standing...and then the light becomes so bright that when he turns Ryan can see right inside the small cave the river has carved out of the bank.

"Oh God! Please let her be alive. Dear God help me!"

The river has obviously run into the cave at some point, it's wet and cold as ice. "Shenna...Shenna open your eyes...please Shenna, open your eyes."

His hand is on her carotid artery trying to find a pulse but he feels nothing and she's as blue as blue can be. Taking off his jacket he wraps it about her then carries her back into the river.

"Now what...I can't make it back up the bank!" Ryan shouts, but he can no longer see the man on the opposite river bank.

Fighting against the current, Ryan begins to walk up river to where he knows the bank is lower. Then a miracle happens and he just has to go with the flow no matter that he can't believe his own eyes.

Two boulders roll towards him, the smaller stopping in front of him and the slightly larger one settling behind it. It only takes a second for Ryan to see the plan and then the light is back, only now it's coming from above his head.

Using the rocks as steps Ryan carries Shenna, who mysteriously now weighs nothing at all, up to the top of the bank and to safety. There Ryan sees a man he recognises from the photo's in Shenna's lounge. "Thank you...for loving Shenna enough to help me find her."

The intensive care unit is a scary place for a child, but Ryan feels that Neirin is intelligent enough to cope. He has explained what the boy can expect to see and how his mum will look.

Sitting by his mother's bedside, Neirin holds her hand talking to Shenna about nothing in particular, like he's having a conversation and has no doubt at all that she can hear him.

Ryan isn't so sure. He wants to believe – the

doctors say it's a miracle that Shenna survived at all, but she still has a very long way to go. A ventilator is doing Shenna's breathing for her and an inflatable blanket that the nurses call a bear-hugger is being used to slowly bring her temperature back up. The monitors blip and bleep, and there are IV lines going into the veins in her arms and a large group of them going into the side of her neck.

He's never seen anything like it. Every few minutes the nurses are putting one drug or another into Shenna – he doesn't ask what they are or what they're for...he just waits for the slightest sign that she is improving.

Neirin is still living with Gail; Ryan hasn't left Shenna's side since she was admitted two days ago. Carl brought him a change of clothes in and he's been having hospital meals delivered to the room so that he never has to leave Shenna alone.

He wouldn't have bothered, but the nursing staff threatened to evict him from Shenna's private room if he didn't start taking care of himself, even though he's the one paying the bills.

He'd have offered all his money to the doctor who could save Shenna's life if he thought it would make a difference. But all he can do now is sit with her, hold her hand and pray – something he's never tried before.

"Mr Tempest," the Consultant who is in charge of Shenna's care has come into the room, "how are you doing?"

"I'm fine, more to the point, how's Shenna doing?" Ryan knows he sounds snappy, but what the hell do they expect.

"Mrs Williams appears to be doing as well as anyone has a right to expect of her after such an ordeal. However, we feel it's time to turn off the sedation and allow her to slowly wake up."

"Wake up!" Looking from Shenna to the Consultant and back again, Ryan is not at all sure he's heard right. "You want Shenna to wake up with that tube still in her mouth!" Ryan is alarmed and at full alert now. "Won't she choke on it, gag or something?"

"No, Mr Tempest, she won't." The Consultant pulls up a visitor's chair to sit, although he's on the opposite side of the bed he is now at eyelevel with Ryan. "We do this all the time, Mr Tempest. We need to know if Mrs Williams is asleep because of the medication or due to some other cause."

Frowning over at him, Ryan looks at the

Consultant like he's suddenly grown an extra head. "You told me you were putting Shenna to sleep so that she wouldn't fight that machine," and Ryan shoots out a hand to point to the ventilator. "Now you're telling me that maybe she wouldn't have woken up anyway...so what the hell does that mean?"

This is a bloody nightmare – what the hell's going on? I can't think, damn it! I just can't think!

Usually confident and fully in charge of himself and those around him, Ryan is having a tough time holding it together.

"Maybe we should take this conversation somewhere else," the Consultant nods towards Shenna and Ryan stands to follow him out of the room. "My office is just along here."

When he takes a seat in the Consultant's office, Ryan doesn't notice the size or luxurious appointments, he is focused on just one thing, "Now tell me what you couldn't tell me in Shenna's room – is she dying...is that it?!" This is bad! This is really, really bad, I just know it! God damn it Shenna, you can't leave me now that I know I love you – you just can't bloody leave me!

Watching the worry play out on Ryan's face, the

Consultant moves to pour out two cups of strong coffee. "Milk and sugar...?" he asks, but Ryan just shakes his head. Placing the cup and saucer in front of him, the Consultant retakes his seat placing his own coffee on his desk. "I'm not going to pretty this up for you...I don't believe you need or would appreciate that," he tells Ryan and takes a sip of his coffee. "From what you told us, and from what we determined from examining her during admission, Mrs Williams suffered a prolonged period of exposure to extreme cold," and he watches Ryan nod in agreement. "The examination also showed bruising consistent with physical abuse - do you remember me discussing this with you after we got Mrs Williams admitted to the Intensive Care Unit?"

Thinking back, and it seems like a very long time ago, Ryan pulls out a memory of some such conversation. "Not clearly, but yes I remember that we talked." I talked to a lot of people, doctors, nurses and God knows who else!

"Ok, well I'll try to refresh your memory." Opening Shenna's medical notes, the Consultant first browses the admission notes then looks up at Ryan. "Mrs Williams was critical on admission – quite frankly I have never known anyone to survive the level of hypothermia that she suffered." Stopping to gauge Ryan's ability to take in and understand the information he's being given, the Consultant decides to plough on. "It appears that her body shut down to such an extent that a state of virtual suspended animation was achieved, using only the barest bodily functions to survive." Taking a sip of his coffee to allow that information to sink in, the Consultant waits for a barrage of questions but receives none. "Ok, do I take it that you understand that term?" and when Ryan nods he continues. "As I said, I've never known anyone to survive this level of hypothermia – the problem being that we don't know how starved the brain was of oxygen during this time and hence what Mrs Williams' higher brain function is likely to be."

"Shenna is not going to be a cabbage!" Ryan stands slowly; pushing back his chair he looks at the Consultant with iron determination. "I'll pay whatever it costs to get the best treatment, now you just see that she gets it!"

The Morphine and Midazolam are turned off, other drugs continue to be given but none are causing the continuing state of unconsciousness. After three days and nights of not daring to leave

Shenna's side in case she wakes up alone, Ryan is exhausted and falls asleep with his head resting on her bed and his arm across her lower body.

When Shenna begins to emerge from the darkness she is confused and frightened, not sure where she is or who has taken her. When she tries to call out, Shenna finds that she can't and has no idea why.

A nurse comes into the room just as Ryan wakes and becomes aware of Shenna's movements. She is distressed and trying to pull the tube out of her mouth.

"Shenna...Shenna...you're safe," the nurse tells her while restraining Shenna's hands to stop her from extubating herself, "...you're in the hospital – Ryan Tempest found you and brought you to The Queens Med'."

Shenna's eyes are now wide and searching...then they settle on Ryan and the fear instantly leaves them. Tears slide down the side of her face but Ryan just kisses them all away. Oh Ryan, thank God you're here...

Very carefully Ryan leans over the bed and holds Shenna while she shakes with fear, shock and blessed relief.

"Can this come out now?" he asks indicating the

tube that still attaches Shenna to the ventilator.

But the nurse shakes her head, "I'm going to call your consultant and he will be along to review Mrs Williams – if he's happy then we'll remove the tube, but he may want to hold off on that if he isn't confident that she will be able to breathe adequately on her own."

Holding his hand Shenna calms and tries not to worry Ryan further. A few moments later and her eyelids are too heavy to stay open. Not able to fight it, Shenna sinks into sleep but wakes briefly on and off as if reassuring herself that she is safe and that Ryan is right there with her.

It's lunch time before Shenna is able to wake properly. The Consultant has already been in to assess her breathing and left instruction with the nurse to extubate as soon as Mrs Williams is appropriate.

Asking Ryan to wait outside the room, the nurse removes Shenna's tube and replaces it with a facemask attached by a small flexible length of tubing to an oxygen supply on the wall.

Shenna tries to speak, to thank the nurse, but finds her voice croaky at best and her throat is sore from where the tube has been.

When Ryan returns she immediately holds out her arms and Ryan gladly moves into them and returns her hug tenfold.

The nurse tidies up then discretely leaves them alone.

Two days later Shenna is discharged from hospital apparently none the worse for her traumatic experience. She still has some bruising but it is fading and patchy.

No sooner has she made it through her own front door than the police arrive wanting to question her.

"Alright, damn it," Ryan grudgingly allows the detective and a constable in, "but you will stop the minute Shenna starts to tire!"

God damned police...couldn't they have given her a day of peace before dragging this all up again!

"Mrs Williams, I'm Detective Brent and this is Constable Becket," holding out his hand to Shenna she shakes it then indicates the settee for them to sit, "we need to ask you a few questions to enable us to continue our investigation into your abduction."

"I understand but I don't think there's really much I can tell you." Looking up at Ryan with worried eyes he comes to sit on the arm of her chair and takes her hand.

"Sometimes it's just a tiny detail that helps us to do our job," Detective Brent assures her. "Can you tell us anything about the night you were abducted?"

Brows drawn together Shenna closes her eyes to pull the memories back to the forefront of her mind.

"There was chaos, it was the middle of the night I think, and there was an explosion," she looks up at Ryan who nods and gives her hand a reassuring squeeze. "I was looking out of the bedroom window; Ryan was running towards the dig site, the port-a-cabin was burning furiously and...and there were lots of mini explosions – I was worried someone would be hurt...then I felt a sickening pain at the back of my head..." Her voice tails off and her free hand reaches up to feel the place where someone had struck her into unconsciousness.

"What is the next thing you remember – not just what you saw but what you heard and smelt?" the Detective asked.

"Cold...shivering...so much pain...all over me...my hands and feet were bound and something was tied across my mouth and there was a hood of some sort over my head – I couldn't see anything," rubbing a hand over her forehead Shenna tries not to feel the emotions behind the memories, but it is hard.

"Someone kicked me, more than once I think...Oh God, Neirin...Neirin...she's got him...he's screaming...she's hurting him..." looking up at Ryan her eyes are filled with terror, "...we...we have to find him...we...we..." she can't breathe, her chest is so tight with fear that she almost passes out.

"That's enough," Ryan explodes, moving to lift Shenna into his arms he carries her up to their bedroom. "Just rest Shenna. Neirin is safe with Gail, she's bringing him home this evening to give you time to get settled."

"B.but I heard him...he was screaming in pain and the man kept saying that it was all my fault..."

Stroking her hair, Ryan notices the change in her description of her abductor. "Downstairs, you said 'she's got him' but just now you said 'the man'," Ryan points out quietly. "Try to just concentrate on that, not anything else and see if you can remember if it was a man or a woman who took you."

Outside the bedroom door the detective is listening with interest and making notes.

"I.I don't know why I said she, the voice sounded like a man...but..."

"Don't worry about it now, just get some rest..."

But the detective has stepped into the room and

interrupts. "Stay calm and just think about the person who took you – something made you think it was a woman despite the male voice?" he states boldly moving to the end of the bed.

"Yes...but I don't know what it was...and his voice...there was something wrong...," Shenna went silent and tries to think back to what she had thought at the time, "...it didn't sound human...well it did," she sighs embarrassed, "but it didn't sound normal." Lifting her hands in the air she lets them fall to her side in a helpless gesture.

"Not to worry," Detective Brent assures her, "I want you to forget all about that person and concentrate on your surroundings, what could you hear or smell or feel?"

"I couldn't feel much because my hands were tied," Shenna explains, "although I knew the floor I was laying on was hard and cold, something like concrete or tiles...I don't know."

"Ok, that's good, what else?"

"When the outside door opened I could smell fields, grass and...and something that reminded me of animals...I don't know why..."

"A farm perhaps?" Detective Brent suggests.

"Yes...yes," Shenna's eyes light up and she sits up

with Ryan's help, "I think that's it...and there was a lot of traffic noise sometimes...I remember thinking that they were probably on their way home not realising that I was laying there...dying...listening to them and wishing that I could go home too." It was hell...to be so close to people living their normal lives and knowing that I never would...

Tears begin to slide down her cheeks unnoticed by Shenna.

"You've been a great help, Mrs Williams," Detective Brent tells her softly. "I know we can seem like bullies sometimes, but we need to get the information before the memories are repressed – we have a lot to work on now, thank you." He smiles and begins to leave the room.

"Thank you Detective," Shenna smiles, "I know you have a job to do and I want to help you any way I can – I don't believe any of us will be safe until you catch this man." I can't go through that again and never want Neirin or Ryan to ever know that kind of pain or fear!

Detective Brent nods, "With your permission I'd like to leave Constable Becket with you – she won't question you unless you think of something that you want her to know," he tells her. "Memories can come back at the strangest moments – as well as that, I believe a police presence will put off any further attempts on your life."

Ryan was about to object but when he considers the proposal he can see it makes sense. "Will that be a twenty-four hour presence?"

"With your agreement, yes," Detective Brent confirms.

"I'll need to make up the spare room," Shenna says, then tries to get out of bed.

"I'm perfectly capable of making up a bed," Ryan states sternly, "just rest for a little while longer."

Back in the sitting room, Ryan asks the Detective honestly what the chances of catching this maniac are. "And will they serve a good long sentence?" he adds quietly so as not to be overheard by Shenna.

"That they will," Detective Brent assures him. "We have all sorts of charges to slap him with, not least of which is kidnap and attempted murder."

Breathing out a heavy sigh, Ryan rubs his tired face. "I'm sorry about before," he apologises sincerely, "I just can't bear to see her any more distressed, she's been through enough."

Giving a nod of understanding, Detective Brent gives Ryan's arm a gentle pat, "Understandable, completely understandable...but we have some leads to work on now. I'll keep Constable Becket up to date and she'll see to it that you are too."

Opening the front door, Ryan steps aside then follows the detective out to his car. "Is it safe, do you think, for me to go to the dig while your constable is here?" and he indicates the site through the trees. "I mean, she won't leave her alone if I'm not there?" he asks.

"No, not at all – you'll be alright to do what you need to," Detective Brent states confidently. "Constable Becket will be acting as family liaison; I'll be ordering a patrol car stationed outside with two officers at all times. I intend doing that the moment I get in my car."

Letting out another long sigh, this time in relief, Ryan offers his hand to the detective and is pleased when he accepts it. "You've got a hard enough job without me making it more difficult – I'll try not to get in your way in future."

Constable Becket is sat on Shenna's bed, at her request, and is listening to her recalling some disturbing memories. "The child screaming in terror or pain...now I think of it, now that I can think of it, it didn't sound like Neirin – not that I've ever heard him scream like that," Shenna shudders at the thought. "It's just, the tone and pitch when he shouted 'no, please, don't hurt me anymore' it wasn't...it wasn't...I didn't realise he'd said that...I mean...I just remembered hearing him say that..." looking at the female constable, Shenna's head is shaking in confusion. "Is that normal...to just pluck memories out of thin air..." That boy...that poor boy, whoever he was...he was terrified...he was...

"Don't worry, Shenna it's a normal part of the process," Constable Becket assures her. "Things that are too shocking or hurtful can be repressed unconsciously, but in moments of clarity they can surface as flashbacks and can seem quite distressingly real," she warns Shenna. "That's part of the reason Detective Brent wanted me to stay with you – I have training in this area and can help you through the worst of it."

"As well as being on hand to makes notes of any new information she recalls," Ryan interjects from the doorway. Holding up a hand, he steps further into the room, "I'm not complaining, just making an observation – I'm actually glad you're here now that I've had time to think about things." He moves to sit at Shenna's other side. "Detective Brent just told me that there will be two officers stationed in a patrol car outside the house 24/7 until they catch whoever did this." Holding her hand he gives it a gentle squeeze. "And I've just been on the phone to Gail, given her an update and asked her to bring Neirin home in a couple of hours instead of tea-time. I know you won't rest properly until he's home."

Giving Ryan one of her brightest smiles, Shenna thanks him for being so considerate. "You've been so good to us, taken on so much more than I could ever have expected." I love you so very much.

"Having you home safe makes it all worthwhile," and he leans in for a chaste kiss, "just get some rest before Neirin comes home."

Easing down under the duvet Shenna smiles then closes her eyes – she's more tired than she realises and falls asleep almost instantly.

CHAPTER ELEVEN

The farmhouse where Shenna was kept is being wrecked by her abductor. Insanely furious that Ryan Tempest had found Shenna in time to bring her back from the brink of death the kidnapper is taking their fury out on anything they can get their hands on.

"Goddamned woman just won't leave, and when I try to help her on her way a knight in bloody shining armour just has to get in the goddamned way!" A dining chair lands broken with the others, shattered against the wall. Old plates, mugs and anything else that will smash into satisfyingly small pieces are hurled after it until nothing is left to break. But still the fury burns. "Burns...yes...I hate her so much my blood is burning with it," and feeling in their pocket they pull out a lighter and set fire to the splintered wood.

Walking slowly across the field to the hire car they'd pulled off the side of the road and hidden from view, the kidnapper stands to watch the fire catch hold and wishes fervently that Shenna Williams was inside.

"I will make you leave you damned whore...and if Tempest gets in my way I'll take him out too!"

Ryan has been watching out for Gail's car and has come across from the dig to greet them and let them in. He and Gail watch as mother and son hug like they haven't seen each other for months instead of hours and it is heart-warming to see.

"I'll put the kettle on and make you a cuppa if you'd like one," he says to Gail, and she nods with a smile of thanks.

"How are you doing?" Gail asks Shenna when Neirin finally lets her go. "Anything you need me to get you from the shops or washing and ironing that wants doing?"

"You've been an angel already and I can manage the laundry if I take my time," Shenna smiles up at her friend. "I can't thank you enough for what you've done, looking after Neirin so that I didn't have to worry," she tells her, leaving out the bit where she had been frantic that her abductor had also managed to take and torture Neirin. There was no need to spread that particular misery around.

"Juliette was a big help too," Gail admits, "she brought the twins round and watched them all so that I could get caught up on the housework now and then. Though I have to say, the boys were all great together, not a bit of trouble."

Shenna gives a lopsided sceptical grin, "Hmm, a real bunch of angels I'm sure."

Ryan comes in with a cup of tea for Gail and asks Shenna and Constable Becket if they would like a fresh cup.

"No, thank you," the constable replies and Shenna also says, "No thanks, I'm good."

Feeling like a spare part with the three women sat ready to continue their chatter; Ryan hedges his way towards the door and is just about to make his escape when Shenna calls over to him.

"Ryan...is it bad...the damage from the fire...did it destroy all your finds?"

Neirin's head comes up with interest; this is the first he's heard of a fire at the dig.

Looking at Neirin, Ryan grimaces, "We managed

to find some pieces, from the exhibit and from the dig, but a lot of it has been lost I'm afraid."

"I'm sorry Neirin, I forgot that you didn't know about the fire," Shenna tells him, reaching out to take his hand.

"When things are up and running properly again, I'll take you over and we'll just have to work harder to uncover some new finds," Ryan winks at Neirin then says goodbye to the women and goes back to the dig and the cleanup operation that is now in full swing.

"How's everyone doing," Sadie asks him when Ryan arrives back on site, "I wouldn't mind working with Neirin if Shenna is still sleeping?"

"It's good of you to offer, but Shenna is up and Gail is with her as well as the police woman," Ryan explains. "And I don't think Shenna will want to let Neirin out of her sight for a while."

"That's understandable," Carl chimes in as he walks past with his arms full of rubble, "and I'll bet Neirin won't want to be far from Shenna either."

Sadie raises her eyebrows at Carl's back then turns back to Ryan. "Wow...where did that snippet of wisdom come from? I didn't think he had a sensitive bone in his body!"

For the first time in what seems like forever, Ryan gives a genuine grin. "Most men have their sensitive side; they just don't like women to know about it most of the time."

"And they say women are hard to understand," Sadie scoffs good humouredly. "With logic like that it's a wonder anyone ever gets married...or starts going out in the first place. Sheesh!"

Roz puts her head out of the port-a-cabin where she is cleaning up the artefacts that they have managed to retrieve from the rubble. "Were you planning to help in here or just stand out there yammering to the men all day?"

Ryan holds his hands up in mock surrender at the side-on rebuke and heads for his office, leaving Sadie to huff back at Roz with her hands on her hips.

"Getting a bit bossy in your old age...?" Sadie asks Roz as she steps up into the port-a-cabin to help with the clean-up.

"Actually I just wanted to get you in here to show you this," and Roz holds out a compacted piece of earth with round sided objects protruding from it. "I think they are coins," Roz speculates when Sadie turns the object over to inspect it, "and if you look there...I scraped just the tiniest bit...what do you think?"

Moving over to the magnifying lamp, Sadie turns the clod over to take a better look. "Jesus...it looks like gold!"

The girls look at each other with wide eyes then give an excited scream and laugh out loud. "You need to show this to Ryan, it could be a seriously significant find!"

Roz suddenly looks taken aback, "You show him...you're easier with him than I am."

"Don't be stupid..." but Sadie watches as Roz shakes her head and takes a step back, "...oh alright. But you come with me!" And not taking no for an answer, Sadie takes Roz' elbow and marches her over to Ryan's office.

When they arrive he is on the telephone, deep in conversation with Detective Brent.

"Ok, thanks for letting me know – I'll go up to the house in a minute to be there when Constable Becket talks with Shenna...it's bound to be distressing for her." Nodding, Ryan gets to his feet then spots the girls at the port-a-cabin door and waves them in. "Ok, Detective, I'll bear that in mind, goodbye."

Letting out a long breath Ryan looks at the girls with worried eyes.

"We can come back..." Roz offers already taking a step towards the door.

"No, no, you're here now," and taking a seat at his desk Ryan tries to hide the strain he is under by giving them an interested smile, "just tell me it's good news and I'm all yours."

Roz feels her knees go weak and her mouth turn dry just at the thought. But Sadie is more forthright and openly excited.

"Take a look," and she hands the clod over to Ryan for him to examine.

Getting up, he walks over to his own magnifying lamp and, as Sadie had, turns the lump of compacted soil over in his hands to examine it. Then, without saying a word, he picks up a small bladed tool and begins to carefully scrape away at the surface.

Turning to smile at them, Ryan holds out the clod where a chunk of it has fallen away. "This is a gold coin of the Roman rebel emperor, Magnus Maximus circa 383 to 388. He was a Roman general who successfully defeated an invasion by the Picts, who lived in Scotland, but then weakened the defences of Britain by setting off for Gaul with his troops to make his bid to become emperor. " His grin is wide and makes his blue eyes sparkle. "I think it's fairly safe to assume that the other two will turn out to be the same or coins of a similar time period, as they were obviously stored together."

"That is amazing," Sadie's eyes have gone wide and she turns to smile at Roz, "and you found them."

"Well...I...it was the bomber who found them really," Roz flusters and blushes. "When Carl and Paul hauled the port-a-cabin wreckage out of the way there was at least a two foot deep crater in the ground. I was rummaging to find the exhibits and other artefacts when I came across that," and she points at the clod Ryan is still holding.

"Well...I'm loathe to thank that maniac for anything, but it looks like that incident did us a good turn." Then his face pales and he hurriedly takes it back. "That was a callous thing to think let alone voice out loud – I don't want you to mention anything like that ever. And definitely not around Neirin or Shenna...ok!" Bloody hell! How could you even think that!

"No, of course not," Sadie confirms, "we knew you didn't mean it like that anyway." And Roz nods enthusiastically in the background.

"Jesus...what a bloody mess!" Rubbing both hands over his strained face and pushing them back through his overlong hair, the girls can't remember ever seeing him look so bad. "I have to get up to the cottage," he tells them and stands abruptly. "I don't know how long I'll be, but I will definitely make it back before you all turn in." He looks from one girl to the other and tries to smile. "You've both been real troopers – this hasn't been a typical dig in any sense of the word – but you've been great. Now don't put yourselves in any danger by going off on your own – you stick with the lads until this maniac is caught." He looks over at the two security guards who are covering the day shift. "And don't forget to feed the security; you look after them and they'll look after you that much better."

When he lets himself into the cottage a few minutes later Ryan can see that Constable Becket hasn't yet imparted her news to Shenna, as she is reading happily with Neirin on the settee. Gail, he knew, had left over an hour since; he'd watched her car drive away.

Looking up, Shenna smiles a greeting that tilts his heart with the simple pleasure of seeing her. "How have you been?" Ryan takes a seat on the settee next to her and Neirin.

"I'm fine, stop worrying, you have enough to do getting the dig back on track." Shenna places a hand over his and gives his fingers a gentle squeeze.

Her hand feels so small and frail on his; and this

time his heart contracts with pain at the thought of what she has been through. And now he is here to help Shenna bear up to some difficult news that could seriously knock her back.

"Neirin, would you mind playing in your room for a while," Constable Becket smiles encouragingly, "I need to discuss a few things with your mum."

With a frown, Neirin shuffles off the settee then stands looking at the police officer. "I don't want you to make her cry," then he turns to Ryan with a pleading look that tears his heart in two. "You won't let her make my mummy cry, will you? I don't want her to be upset anymore."

At that moment, it didn't matter that Neirin had an advanced intelligence that made him older than his years; he was just a little boy who didn't want his mummy to be upset.

Ryan holds a hand out and waits for Neirin to take it. "I'm here, Neirin, and I won't let anything happen to upset your mum – do you believe me?"

Neirin looks deep into his clear blue eyes and decides that he does. With a nod he pulls his hand free and walks towards the stairs. "Dad will tell me if you do!" he shoots back at Constable Becket before running up the stairs to his room.

Looking from Neirin to Shenna and Ryan on the settee, Constable Becket raises a questioning brow.

"It's nothing," Shenna dismisses easily then returns the constables questioning look. "What is this about," looking up at Ryan she can see that he knows something, "and why are you home?" Then she pales visibly and her hands clasp together over her heart. "He's back...another animal...or a note...or..." Oh please, no more...no more...

"No!" Ryan snaps out to stop the hysteria that is rising in Shenna. "Now stay calm, for Neirin's sake."

Looking up at him with wide fearful eyes, Shenna finds herself drawing on his strength to reign in the fear. "Yes...yes, you're right, I can do this," but her fingers, which have taken hold of his hand, are now locked firm in his.

"We need to make you aware that the farmhouse where you were held has been badly burned in an arson attack," Constable Becket tells Shenna quietly, calmly. "We know it was the place where you were held because a few items were found which confirm that." Giving Shenna a moment to take the enormity of that in, Constable Becket then continues, "It is also possible that you were correct about your abductor being a woman – though that isn't yet confirmed."

"Why, did you find some clothing or female possessions – surely you could get fingerprints or DNA..." Shenna tries to remain calm. Could this be a friend after all – someone I have trusted and cared about whom all along wanted me out...or dead? But who and why?

"We found an electronic gadget that is used to distort the voice of someone who doesn't want to be recognised," Constable Becket informs her. "I'm sure it has its legitimate uses, though I admit I can't think of any, but we have come across similar items before that have been used to commit just this type of crime."

"Then it could still be a man or a woman," Ryan observes flatly. "Even a man wouldn't want his voice recognised, but would it alter a female voice enough to make it sound convincingly male?"

"That's the big question isn't it," the constable affirms. "But you weren't convinced, were you Shenna, not fully convinced?"

"I need to think." Shenna pushes up from the settee looking distracted. "I'm going to make some tea, would either of you like some?"

Ryan gives a slight shake of his head and looks nonplussed by her question but the constable just says, "Yes please – need any help?"

"No, that's fine; I just want to think a while."

Waiting for Shenna to disappear into the kitchen, Ryan looks at the constable for an explanation.

"It's a common reaction. Doing something inane and ordinary helps to focus the mind while giving the hands something to do," she tells him quietly. "You may find this isn't the last time Shenna will use such tactics, just keep an eye on her and allow her to do whatever she needs to, to focus on what her mind is trying to recall."

"So, she may get up at three in the morning and just start ironing?" he asks sceptically.

"Actually, that's a classic...or cleaning the house from top to bottom," she smiles brightly making her look much younger than her austere uniform usually allows.

Looking much calmer and a lot more in control, Shenna brings back two cups of tea with sugar and milk already in the constable's cup, just as she knows she likes it.

Settling back down next to Ryan, Shenna takes a sip of her tea then ploughs right in. "An electronically altered voice fits in with the unreal quality that has been niggling at me," she explains, "and the recording of the child screaming also sounded strange – possibly for the same reason. But I'm not sure about that...maybe I was looking for reasons to reassure myself that it wasn't Neirin after all...I don't really know." And maybe I just don't want to remember...don't want to keep hearing that child screaming for me to help him. "Who was the child?"

For a moment both Ryan and the constable look confused, then the constable says, "We found a tape recorder in what would have been the lounge, but it was badly melted and there was nothing salvageable. However, we believe it may have been an edited version of a children's playground – they scream and play at the tops of their voices and the words were probably spliced together to form the sentence that you heard – another plausible explanation of why it didn't sound quite right."

"That...is...possible and downright diabolical!" Shenna finishes angrily. "To think the innocence of children could be used in such a way is sickening." A flush of temper comes to her cheeks and Ryan is actually relieved to see it. "If I ever get my hands on the person who did this..." I can't know this monster - anyone that cruel and callous wouldn't be able to hide their true nature all of the time...there would be tells.

The constable raises a cautionary hand. "Let's not go there – you don't want to say anything that might get you into trouble later," she warns affably but clearly. "I need to ask you a couple of questions, and at the same time give you some more information – are you ready?"

She was more than ready now that her dander was up. "Ask away, I'm not afraid anymore, damn him to hell!"

Fighting talk and the constable takes advantage while she can but knows that it probably won't last. "Have you ever been to the Abbot's farm, it's just the other side of the forest and has a dirt track leading from the main road?"

"I used to take Neirin there when he was two. Frank Abbot was so good with him and let him see the animals," then Shenna frowns and gasps. "That was the smell I thought I knew – we were there often before Frank fell ill, then he had to move into a nursing home to be cared for." Putting a hand to her forehead and closing her eyes, Shenna drags back the memories, old and new. "He kept goats, in pens near the house – they have a smell all their own and that's what came through the door every time someone opened it." Shaking her head, Shenna recalls being on that stone cold floor and wondering about that familiar smell.

Oh, Frank, I hope you never hear of this, it would break your heart.

"And the house is gone?" she asks the constable. "Didn't you say that it was set on fire?"

"I don't believe it's completely unsalvageable – from what I've heard it was a well-built stone house but some of the timbers have been badly damaged and any wood floors, furniture, window frames and doors have all gone." The constable readies herself to tell Shenna the more shocking news. Finishing her tea she places the cup and saucer on a nearby table. "We found the remains of your clothing in a small room off the main kitchen, it was barely touched by the fire and that's also where we found the electronic voice box and a few other items." Taking a steadying breath, Constable Becket continues, "We also found blood splatter and drag marks that lead all the way over to the woods between your property and the farm. They aren't so clear in the woods, apparently, but Detective Brent said the dogs were able to follow the scent right to the edge of the river where Mr Tempest found you."

"Shit!" It is Ryan's turn to suffer the traumatic

flashbacks to memories he'd just as soon forget. I'll never forget that night – for as long as I live I'll never get the image of Shenna stuffed carelessly into that shallow cave...I thought she was dead...she was so blue...so cold...

"It's alright, Ryan...I'm right here," Shenna tells him and touches his cheek with gentle fingers, "and I'm safe...thanks to you."

"But you so nearly weren't...if it wasn't for Cade..." He breaks off, suddenly aware that he is thinking out loud.

A silence hangs over them and Constable Becket decides not to break it.

It is Shenna who speaks first. "You...you saw Cade?" she asks when Ryan doesn't continue. I should have known...Cade, always taking care of us.

"I don't know what I saw," he snaps uncharacteristically, "I was half out of my mind with worry and probably imagined the whole thing."

"But you don't really think so...?" Constable Becket put in quietly.

"Just leave it," he snaps again, "it has nothing to do with the case and can't possibly help in any way."

"Forgive me, but you have no idea of what can be useful in a case," the young constable persists bravely. "Why don't you just tell us what happened and let me be the judge of what is useful?"

Pushing up from the settee, Ryan stands tall and rigid and totally uncompromising. "Because I don't really know what happened and I sure as hell don't believe what I think happened." Then he turns abruptly heading for the stairs. "And Neirin has been on his own for quite long enough," he states, heading up to the boy's room without looking back. This is crazy...maybe I'm crazy – I sure as hell was that night!

Giving a knock on the door, he waits until Neirin shouts for him to come in. "How did you know it was me...?" Then Ryan remembers what Shenna has told him about Neirin's conversations with his dad. "Oh, your dad – is he still here?"

Looking at Ryan with an assessing gaze, Neirin tells him, "You don't sound like mum when she asks me that question."

Taking a seat on the boy's bed, Ryan asks, "So, how does your mum sound when she asks you about your dad?"

Chuckling, Neirin smiles conspiratorially up at Ryan. "Like she thinks I've gone crazy but doesn't want to let on."

Ruffling Neirin's hair playfully Ryan laughs at the boy's candour. "Well we know different, don't we?"

"You've spoken to dad, haven't you, or seen him – I don't think mum ever has, that's why she doesn't believe," he states sagely.

"He helped me to save your mum's life," Ryan tells him, shocking himself by doing so. Yes, he did, he really did...however crazy that sounds.

But Neirin isn't upset by the revelation. "I wondered if he did something – no one was able to find mum, then the minute everyone was gone...you did," Neirin smiles brightly. "I think it's great that you and dad like each other – maybe that's why he said it's ok for me to call you dad now?"

"You think? Well, maybe you want to think about that some more – it wouldn't hurt my feelings if you wanted to call me Ryan."

Feeling suddenly uncertain, Neirin looks down at his hands in his lap. "Aren't you and mum getting married anymore?"

Damn and blast, you idiot! "We are getting married the minute your mum is up to it," Ryan states firmly and puts an arm around Neirin's shoulders, pulling him into his side. "I just don't want you to feel that it's expected of you to call me dad – not that I wouldn't be incredibly honoured by it if you did."

"Ok," Neirin relaxes and then giggles. "Does getting married mean having babies?"

Stunned for a moment, Ryan takes a second or two to think about that. "What would you think if we did want to have a baby?"

"I'd get to be a big brother and I could share my tools and show them how to dig carefully," Neirin answers with an excited flourish. "And I'd help mum so that she can still do lessons and me and the baby can have lessons together..."

"Slow down," Ryan laughs at his enthusiasm, but is delighted all the same. "Let's get the wedding in the bag first, then we can think about the future – our future," and he gives Neirin's shoulders another hug. What a thought...our future...our baby...my baby...

CHAPTER TWELVE

For a while the misery of the last weeks is forgotten. Shenna enlists Gail and Juliette into helping her prepare for a small wedding. They are delighted by the news and are eager to take Shenna wedding shopping.

"You're going to need a dress, even if you marry in a registry office," Juliette tells her when Shenna pooh-pooh's the idea. "And there's nothing to say you can't have a proper church wedding – you're a widow not a divorcee!"

"And you're so in love it's written all over the pair of you," Gail put in her two-penneth.

Blushing scarlet, Shenna has to smile. "Yes, well, that's as maybe, but I don't think Ryan wants anything ostentatious."

"But you haven't asked him – maybe he thinks you want to play it down?" Juliette suggests. "Things are different now; maybe you should talk about it and see how you both feel, before you lose the opportunity."

They have gone back to having dinner together in the evenings. Shenna has cooked and served a chilli-con-carne, but she is pushing it distractedly around her plate rather than eating it.

"Are you going to tell us what's on your mind," Ryan asks eventually, having given up waiting for Shenna to volunteer anything.

"Sorry…?" Shenna looks up in a daze realising that Ryan has said something.

Giving a roll of his eyes to Neirin, Ryan asks her again, "I said, are you going to tell us what's on your mind – it's obvious something is you've barely eaten any of this lovely meal."

"Oh," she smiles, "I'm glad you're enjoying it – it's my own recipe."

Letting his knife tap, tap, slowly on his plate, Ryan waits patiently.

"Ok, ok," Shenna cringes inwardly and blushes to the roots of her hair. "I went over to Juliette's house with Gail today," she begins to explain, "and they wanted me to go dress shopping." Shenna waits, hoping that Ryan will cotton on, but he just sits listening expectantly. "They wanted me to go dress shopping," she repeats agitatedly, then sags in her seat when Ryan continues to look blank. "Wedding dresses, they wanted to take me shopping for a wedding dress!"

Constable Becket, now fondly known as Beccy - which had caused a lot of amusement when they had all found out that her name was Rebecca Becket and that she had been teased at school being called Beccy Becket over and over by the boys – was now a fixture in the household and sat opposite Neirin at the dining table trying her hardest not to smile. She had, of course, been with Shenna when her friends had suggested talking to Ryan about a church wedding, now she is watching Shenna flounder in an attempt to do just that.

"Doesn't that sound a little excessive for a registry office," Ryan asks quite seriously. "Though women know more about these things than men – you should go with what you want, Shenna. If you'd like a wedding dress then that's what you shall have."

She feels like getting up and bashing her forehead against the brick wall. This is getting painful...just ask him you coward! "I...I was wondering how you might feel, given that things are different now, and we might want to look back on the memories more fondly...I just thought...perhaps...a church...wedding..." Oh bloody, bloody, bloody hell!

Beccy, who has her head bent low over her dinner plate, is almost in tears trying not to laugh and is biting heroically on her knuckles.

Ryan actually chokes on the mouthful of mince he's just put in his mouth and Beccy shoots up to slap his back hard. "Thank you...," he manages eventually then notices the teeth marks on her knuckles. "Didn't you like the meal...?"

"Oh...it's been great so far," she smiles then chuckles tellingly.

"Hmm, so you're all a party to this?" and he narrows his eyes in Neirin's direction.

"Not me," Neirin declares honestly, "I don't know a thing."

"It was just an idea that Gail and Juliette had," Shenna has paled now, appalled that Ryan had such a strong reaction to the idea of marrying her in a church. Maybe I've got this whole thing all wrong. He hasn't exactly come right out and said that he loves me...but then neither have I.

"So...it wasn't your idea as well?" he asks quietly.

It had been funny to listen to Shenna flounder so badly, but now Beccy feels like an intruder in a very private family conversation. The main meal is mostly over now so she takes her own and Neirin's empty plate into the kitchen.

Neirin takes the hint and follows her out. "Do you think they are going to argue?" he asks Beccy anxiously.

Bending down to eyelevel, Beccy smiles and explains, "I know you've never lived with a mum and a dad before, but you're going to have to get used to the idea that they will argue sometimes. However, that doesn't necessarily mean that they are going to go their separate ways," she tells him with a rueful smile. "My parents used to fight like cats and dogs, it was just their way, but they still love each other and seem to enjoy the making up as much as the arguments."

"You said 'used to', don't they argue anymore?"

"Not so much," Beccy gives a loving chuckle, "they seem to have mellowed over the years, but when they do they can still raise the roof, I assure you."

"Ok," Neirin nods though he is still frowning. "So

you think they'll still get married?" he asks looking towards the closed kitchen door.

"I certainly do, don't you?"

"I love Ryan, and I want him to be my new dad so much..."

"But you're frightened of losing him too?" Beccy asks gently.

Biting his bottom lip, Neirin's eyes suddenly fill with tears and he throws his arms around Beccy's neck unable to answer.

At that precise moment Shenna walks in with the rest of the dinner plates and immediately puts them down to come over to Neirin.

"What's wrong, what happened?" Shenna asks full of concern, and on hearing her Ryan follows into the kitchen.

"What's going on?" Ryan echoes Shenna's concern.

But Neirin just clings to Beccy, burying his head in her neck.

Taking Neirin with her, Beccy stands and hugs the boy. "He just got scared," she explains, "he isn't used to the idea of arguments or disagreements and thought maybe you wouldn't get married after all."

"That does it," Ryan huffs with conviction, "we're

getting married as soon as it can be arranged and if you want that to be in a church, so be it, that's fine by me," he tells Shenna. Then he turns to Beccy and holds out his arms to take Neirin. "As for you, young man, I hoped you knew me better than this...I wouldn't leave you or your mum for anything – I love you both too much!" And he hugs Neirin to him and reaches out his other arm to include Shenna in the embrace.

Now she really does feel in the way, so Beccy slides unnoticed from the room and goes through to the lounge to give them some privacy.

Ryan did whatever he could to pull a few strings and got a special license granted for the wedding. Seven days from now and they would be joined as man and wife in a little church on the outskirts of town.

At the same time as getting the license granted, Ryan put the announcement in the local press as well as the main broadsheets. He was so proud to be marrying Shenna and had included a mention of Neirin too, which Shenna loved when he showed it to her.

Finally, after that day in the kitchen, they have

managed to tell each other exactly how they feel. It has been a relief to them both, just to let their feelings out and be able to show them in everyday ways.

"I never thought I could feel this way," Ryan tells Shenna, as they sip a glass of wine together in the late evening, his arm about her shoulders. "My mother screwed up my perspective of love and parenthood, I realise that now. I was determined no woman would ever carry my child – I wouldn't allow them to have power over even the smallest part of me, let alone a child I might be unable to protect."

Her hand brushes over his chest soothingly, "That sounds terribly sad, but understandable from what you've told me of your childhood."

"The weird thing is I thought I hated her...but now I realise I don't." I really mean that...I never thought I would!

"You've got too big a heart to truly hate anyone," she murmurs.

"No," he states suddenly vehement, "don't put me on some pedestal that I'll only fall off of and disappoint you. If I ever find out who hurt you I won't have a problem with ripping his head off his shoulders, I assure you!"

"Ok," Shenna smiles into his chest and kisses him

there, "I'll give you that one – with pleasure. But you know what I mean, just look at the way you are with your crew – you're not just a boss, you care about them and their safety – and you won't convince me that the security guards, who you are paying for out of your own pocket, are only there to protect the site from further vandalism. You care," she asserts firmly, "and I love that you do." I'm so lucky to have you in my life.

Glad that she can't see the embarrassment on his face, Ryan has to concede that she is right, even if it is just to himself. "So, how are the wedding plans coming?" he asks in a hopeful bid to change the subject. "Did you find a dress you are happy with?"

Sitting up to face him, Shenna's smile is radiant and Ryan feels his heart do a back-flip in a way he still hasn't gotten used to.

"I did, it's simple and not too girlie – I'm not exactly a teenage bride," she smiles ruefully, "but I can still step out in style when the occasion demands."

His smile is so full of love that Shenna basks in it delightedly. "You will make a beautiful bride," his hand touches her pink cheek softly, "and I'll be waiting with eager arms to make you my wife."

They were just about to kiss when Beccy came running down the stairs, gun in hand. "Stay there both of you – I'm going to check out back!"

Looking out the front window they see the patrol car with both doors open and no occupants inside.

"Beccy must have radioed them," Ryan suggests. "I feel useless just staying here; I should be out there helping."

Slipping an arm about his waist, Shenna lays her head against his heart and hears the strong galloping beat of it. "No, Ryan – they're trained to deal with this sort of thing, though I must admit I don't like Beccy being out there." Stay with me...stay safe!

"False alarm," Beccy announces ten minutes later. "I don't know what set off the security light, or what the shadow was that I thought I saw in the garden, but there is no sign of an intruder that we can see."

Shenna wants to ask if she is sure, but thinks it might sound insulting. She wants to go out and check for herself; after all who would know better than she if something were out of place.

Instead she just goes into the kitchen and puts the kettle on but can't resist the opportunity to look out of the window.

"Caught you!" Ryan makes her jump when he

comes up behind her. "You want to get out there and look as badly as I do but we'll leave it till morning," he suggests. "Then we'll take a careful look around and see if we can spot something the police didn't."

Beccy must have gotten up especially early. When Ryan and Shenna get downstairs they see her through the lounge window already talking to the two officers in the patrol car.

"Don't you have some washing to put on the line?" Ryan asks, looking for an excuse for them both to go into the back garden. "Or maybe we should go check the chickens – I heard them squawking last night – must have given them a fright."

Giving an amused chuckle, Shenna nods enthusiastically. "We can go egg collecting, that wouldn't be out of the ordinary."

The day is bright with sunshine and warm enough not to bother with jackets.

"I hope it's like this on Friday," Ryan speculates looking up at the perfectly blue sky.

"Mmm, it would make a perfect wedding day," Shenna agrees. It will be perfect no matter what the weather does. You, me and Neirin...that's what will make it perfect!

The chickens allow their eggs to be collected and

Shenna stows them in her basket carefully. Then she places it on top of the coop and helps Ryan look for clues.

There isn't anything obvious, but they continue looking anyway.

"Over here," Ryan calls softly, and waits for Shenna to reach him. "There's a heel print in the soil at the back of this bush and another, shallower one to the side of it – the ground is a bit hard for a toe print but they probably leant on their heels for some time before being disturbed," he suggests.

"Let me see that," Beccy asks having come into the garden unnoticed by either of them.

They move aside and give a quick look that says 'damn, we got caught after all that' across Beccy's back as she bends to take a look at the heel prints Ryan found.

"Well, you could be right," she concedes straightening herself up. "The ground is hard and the heel prints look like the intruder was leant back against the fence and rocking on their heels." Hands on hips, Beccy surveys the rest of the garden. "Notice anything out of place?" she asks Shenna.

Taking her time, Shenna turns in a full circle but nothing catches her eyes. "I don't see anything different, sorry."

"But we know who ever took Shenna is still around," Ryan's voice is soft as granite, and twice as hard, "so that means no going out alone for you or Neirin. No visits to friends without Beccy along, and no overnight stays for Neirin until we catch this bastard!"

Shenna's first instinct is to assert her independence, and Ryan seems to realise that. "I'm asking you, Shenna, for my sanity's sake – I can't go through losing you again!" I may not get you back a second time...I won't allow that to happen...I can't!

Moving to his side, she slips her arm around his waist and gives a gentle hug. "I understand, and I'll keep myself and Neirin safe, don't worry," and she stands on tiptoes to kiss his cheek.

If it weren't for Beccy, Ryan would have pulled her more fiercely into his arms, he wants to feel her close and sink right into her.

"I'd appreciate that," is all he eventually says, but he also returns her hug. I'd appreciate getting my hands around that cowards neck even more, but having you safe will have to do for now.

Back in the cottage Shenna starts breakfast and before long Neirin comes downstairs to join them.

"Beccy, would you mind taking this out to

Detectives Byrnes and Casey?" Putting two mugs of sweet tea on the tray with the bacon sandwiches she's made for their breakfast, Shenna passes it over to Beccy.

"You do know they are all fighting over this job at the station now that word has spread that the food and drink is plentiful and yummy to boot," Beccy laughs as she takes the tray and heads out of the back door.

"Bacon and eggs for you too?" she asks Ryan, and he gives a rueful smile along with a shake of his head.

"After smelling those bacon sandwiches I could certainly eat a few, but I need to get over to the dig and we do our best planning over a meal," he tells her. Turning to Neirin he adds, "Fancy having breakfast over at the dig; I know the crew will be happy to see you?"

Neirin's face breaks into a beaming grin, "Yes please – is that ok mum?"

"I'll keep him with me at all times," Ryan assures her when Shenna looks tense, "and it'll give you some time with Gail and Juliette to finalise any wedding arrangements."

On the way to Gail's an hour later, Shenna asks

Beccy if there has been any progress with the investigation. "I know the farmhouse was badly burned but you did manage to salvage a few things."

"Yes, we did," Beccy confirms, "but I'm afraid nothing positive has come back from forensics as yet." Glancing over at Shenna, Beccy feels for her and wishes she could give her better news. "A couple of crime scene officers are coming over while we're out to take details of the prints in the back garden – I know they didn't look like much but you just never know what will prove important at the end of the day."

"It's ok," Shenna nods agreeably, "I know I just have to be patient...it's just that...knowing it and doing it are very different."

Beccy lives with Shenna and her family twenty-four-seven now. When it came time for the first shift change they hadn't been happy at the thought of someone they didn't know moving in for the next couple of days. The station had agreed to the request and even thought it was a good idea, and Beccy didn't mind in the least – she is single with no ties so living at the cottage didn't pose any personal problems for her.

"Ok," Gail announces when the women are all

seated in her lounge, "let's make a plan of attack. We definitely have to buy the dress and shoes today – you just don't have time to procrastinate on that. Then we need to finalise the bouquet – I know you say you don't want anything too formal but even a bunch of buttercups and daisies take time to arrange."

Maybe it was a release of tension, or maybe it was wedding nerves, but when Shenna starts to laugh she finds she just can't stop and before they know it Beccy, Juliette and Gail are all falling about laughing too.

"Oh boy," Shenna wipes the tears from her cheeks and notices Juliette doing the same, "I haven't had a belly-laugh like that in forever. Really...I can't remember the last time I allowed myself to lose control."

Even Beccy is enjoying the atmosphere, though she is still on duty and soon pulls herself back into line.

"What about Ryan and Neirin, are they already sorted for the wedding?" Gail asks.

"I wanted to buy a suit for Neirin today, but Ryan said that's man's stuff and they're going together to get kitted out tomorrow," Shenna tells them with very different tears in her eyes now. "They are so good together, Neirin asked Ryan if it was alright to call him dad and I could see it meant the world to him and was totally unexpected."

"That is so sweet," Gail and Juliette agree. "You are a very lucky woman to have found two wonderful men to love in one lifetime."

The day of shopping goes well, the women wear out the pavements going from one wedding boutique to another and finalising all the other details that even a small wedding entails – and all the time unaware that they are being watched.

A face in the crowd; a shadow in a doorway; a stealthy movement to blend into the surroundings...not once do they notice that a predator is in their midst, even when Beccy takes a sudden stumble off the curb into the afternoon traffic.

"Christ Beccy, are you alright?!" Gail asks having caught the younger woman's arm and dragged her back.

Pale and shaking, Beccy's eyes dart all around her, "I think it was just the crowd jostling a bit too enthusiastically," she suggests, but frowns at the memory of a hand on the small of her back.

Shenna hears her name being called, "Shenna,

Shenna, are you ok? Oh my gosh!" Roz is stunned and amazed to find no one is hurt.

"Roz? I thought Ryan was keeping you on site until it was safe," Shenna frowns at the younger woman. "Or at least asking one of the boys to tag along if you had to go anywhere?"

Blushing, Roz holds up a Boots' bag, "Girl stuff – didn't really fancy male company when I picked up a few necessary supplies."

Rolling her eyes, Shenna gives a smile, "Sorry, I didn't think to ask if you needed anything – I can always pick up anything you need."

"Well, actually," Roz was squirming awkwardly, "it does feel kind of good to get out on my own. I don't mind company most of the time, but it's been a bit intense lately."

"Ok, but if you're ready to go back we could give you a lift?" Shenna still isn't convinced that it's a good idea for Roz to be out on her own.

"Just a bit longer," Roz shakes her head in reply, "I'm really enjoying some me time."

"Alright," Shenna can't help smiling at the younger woman's obvious enjoyment of playing truant and doing her own thing. "Just keep your eyes open and yourself safe – I'll see you back at the dig site."

With a wave and a smile Roz moves off into the crowd and out of sight.

"Time to go home and get some tea – I don't know about yours but my feet are killing me," Gail tells them and heads for the car park.

When they reach the cars they have parked next to each other the four women stand open mouthed.

In large red letters the word 'WHORE' has been spray painted on the bonnet of Shenna's car.

"Don't touch it," Beccy commands, "I'm going to radio this in and get a team out to see if they can get some prints."

The joy of the day has been well and truly dashed, and Shenna can't take her eyes off the hideous word.

"Come with us," Gail offers, "we'll all go back to mine in my car and the police can do what they have to with yours, Shenna."

She doesn't reply, just stands horrified by the blood red paint that is dripping down the bonnet of her car.

"Maybe we should call Ryan," Juliette suggests, "I've still got his mobile number in my phone from when you had Neirin," she tells Gail.

"That might be the best idea," Gail agrees, and

watches a silent tear trickle down Shenna's cheek.

By the time Ryan arrives the police are taking photos of the car and the immediate surroundings. He finds Shenna, still holding her recent purchases seemingly bemused by the proceedings.

"I'm sorry," he tells her as he wraps Shenna in a protective and loving embrace, "Juliette told me you'd all had an enjoyable afternoon, I'm sorry you had to come back and find this." Looking over the top of Shenna's head his eyes become angry, "What a bloody mess!"

That evening, Shenna is unusually quiet. On Friday she and Ryan are due to get married, but now Shenna is afraid that the nearer the time comes the more danger they are all in.

"She didn't stumble," Shenna suddenly announces to the quiet room. Ryan is reading a newspaper, or attempting to, but even his thoughts are proving too distracting.

"I'm sorry; I don't think I heard you?" Ryan frowns over at Shenna.

"Beccy, she didn't stumble into the road," Shenna turns her head to look at Ryan. "I heard her talking to one of the officers in the car park – she asked him to look at any CCTV in the area that might have caught the incident, and she told him she felt a hand in the small of her back just before she fell forward." Her green eyes appear almost too calm. "Someone pushed her deliberately Ryan, and this time I don't think they were aiming for me...I think they wanted to take Beccy out to clear the field for their next attempt at abducting or...or killing me."

Her voice hasn't wavered or risen and her eyes are steady on his, yet Ryan can feel the tension coming off her in waves. "You've finished everything you need to do for the wedding," he observes just as calmly, "now there's only Neirin and I to sort out. I've already doubled the security at the dig and I've arranged for two more guards to accompany us to get our suits – I'm not leaving anything to chance, Shenna. Nothing!" We will get married and I will protect you and Neirin...somehow.

CHAPTER THIRTEEN

Beccy has already turned in for the night when Shenna and Ryan go up to bed. Before going in to their bedroom they do their nightly check on Neirin and find him sleeping without a care in the world.

An encyclopaedia lies near him on his bed and is open at a basic introduction to archaeology. "I do believe you have a student in the making," Shenna smiles up at Ryan and takes the book from Neirin's bed to replace it on his bookshelf.

Closing the door quietly behind them, they cross the landing to their own bedroom. Shrugging out of her jeans, Shenna stands in a t-shirt and underwear.

Having undressed in double time, Ryan is leaning back in the bed with his hands behind his head watching Shenna move about the room. "You have no idea how sexy you look half undressed like that," he smiles with a wicked glint in his bright blue eyes.

"You look sexy in or out of clothes," Shenna retorts with a roll of her eyes. "Haven't you noticed how Roz drools and hangs on your every word," she teases. "Poor girl, she's got it bad," climbing in beside him Shenna moves into Ryan's arms and glides her hands possessively over his chest then kisses him with outright passion. "Not that I can blame her..." she breaths heavily, "...so do I."

Their lips speak of the depth of their love without uttering a single word; the heat, the taste, the need, all speak for themselves.

Moving over her, Ryan enjoys running his fingers through her lush red hair. He strokes a hand over her cheek and draws his thumb across her lips. They are full and soft and he hasn't tasted them nearly enough yet.

Closing in for another earth shattering kiss, Ryan nibbles on her bottom lip then pushes his tongue between them. Shenna allows him to dominate the kiss, inviting him to plunder and shake the foundations of her world. Her heart is hammering, her breathing ragged and shallow, and the throb between her thighs is becoming unbearable.

Feeling her shift beneath him, Ryan reaches down to cup her and feels the dampness seeping through her panties. A finger slides beneath them, teasing her with just the lightest strokes until her hips lift off the bed demanding more.

That single finger slips inside the moist heat and brings her to a devastating climax that causes a deep moan of release to pass from her lips into Ryan's mouth.

Nudging her thighs apart he moves between them to kneel over Shenna. Removing her bra Ryan tosses it aside and gazes down at her with naked lust in his eyes.

Cupping both breasts he watches her green eyes darken with desire as he moulds them with his large hands. His thumbs tease the nipples, grazing them with his nails then he lowers to sooth with his tongue.

Shenna's back is bowed off the bed, her body a quiver of sensation and need. When he moves his lips down her body she sucks in a breath and holds it. When his tongue pushes into her navel she lets it out in a gasp of unexpected pleasure.

Hands on his shoulders, Shenna holds on as she

feels him move even further down the bed. His tongue should be classed as a lethal weapon she decides, as he uses it to slowly taste and tease the rest of the way down her body.

When he kisses her through her panties Shenna is almost undone. His teeth graze over her again and again then his tongue slips beneath them and finds the tiny pearl of pleasure, flicking over it with rapid strokes he drives her wild.

"Ryan..." Her cry is fuel to his fire and his tongue moves inside her. She is so responsive to his touch; they are good together in every way.

He is throbbing with need and hard as iron but he doesn't rush the pleasure of taking her. He has never known what it is to love a woman so absolutely, and now that he does he treasures such moments for what they truly are; the mating of body, heart, mind and soul.

Panties removed, he pushes inside her, slowly but deeply, he settles himself to keep control. Shenna can sense his need, anticipates the frantic thrusts and is completely undone by his gentleness.

His lips take hers softly, tenderly, his fingers brushing her cheeks. He moves inside her with long slow strokes, "I love you Shenna...with all my heart."

Reaching up a hand to touch his face, Shenna repeats the words back to him, "I love you Ryan, with everything that I am."

Gazing deep into each other's eyes their passion builds and their bodies move in a rhythm as old as time. When her breath catches and her body quivers, Ryan pushes home more forcefully and takes them both over the edge of wonder and delight.

A tear of pure love slides from Shenna's eyes as she embraces the man who has brought her such joy. Cradling his head to her breasts she simply loves him and feels honoured to know that he loves her too.

"I'm a different man since I met you, Shenna," he tells her quietly, his deep voice rumbling into the dark silence of their room. "Thank you for loving me and for allowing Neirin to love me – I'll do whatever I can to be a good dad for him, I promise to take care of you both...always."

Their wedding day dawns bright with sunshine and warmth with not a cloud to mar the blue sky. Shenna and Beccy are alone at the cottage, though the two detectives are still stationed outside in a patrol car.

"Are you sure you don't want me to help you into your dress?" Beccy asks while fussing around Shenna as a wedding attendant should. "I don't mind, and I could make sure it doesn't ruin your hair?"

"The best thing you could do for me right now," Shenna chuckles patiently, "is to put the kettle on and make a nice strong cup of tea."

"Are you sure?" Beccy's voice goes up a couple of octaves in panic. "What if you spill it down your dress?"

"Tea, Beccy...it really is just what I need," Shenna looks in the mirror and over her shoulder to the young woman hovering behind her.

"Are you nervous?" Beccy's blue eyes look back at her in the mirror as Shenna considers the question.

"Amazingly...no, I don't think I am," she smiles surprised. "I'm just excited to get to the church and take our vows – they're not just words, Beccy, we love each other very much and I just want to show him that in the most profound way I know how."

"I think it's lovely," and Beccy gives a sniff as she turns to leave and go make the tea.

Just as Shenna removes the cover on her dress, her mobile rings and she can see that it's Ryan. Her heart gives a joyful leap and her smile turns into an ear to ear grin.

"Hello..."

"It's me," Ryan states unnecessarily, "I just wanted to check you haven't changed your mind."

Hearing the tension in his voice Shenna knows Ryan is only half joking. "I'm so glad you called me...the cottage is empty without you and Neirin around..." she tells him softly, whispering intimately, "...I'm just relieved to hear the sound of your voice."

Remaining silent for a moment, Ryan has to steady his emotions, "I've missed you too, more than I could have imagined."

"Just another hour..." she tells him, all the longing evident in those three little words.

"Yes..." he smiles, and she can hear it in his voice, "...just one more hour till you become Mrs Shenna Tempest." Again Ryan falls silent and Shenna senses his struggle. "I love you, Shenna. I never thought I would dare to trust my heart to a woman's keeping, but it's yours now, there's no going back for me."

Forgetting her makeup and overcome with love for this wonderful man, Shenna allows a few tears fall. "I'll keep it safe," she tells him, "as I know you will mine, and we'll both learn to trust our love as it grows with time."

Ryan gives a cough and has to pull himself together as Neirin enters the room. "It's your mum," she hears him tell Neirin, "would you like to speak to her?" Before he hands his mobile to Neirin he tells Shenna that he will see her soon.

"Hi mum, are you getting ready...we've got our suits on and Ryan says we look exactly alike," Neirin tells her excitedly.

"How did you like staying in the hotel...is your room nice?"

"It's great, Ryan took me for dinner in the restaurant and they had all kinds of puddings and I had chocolate fudge cake with ice-cream," he tells her with obvious enjoyment. "And even when we went back to the room, they have this tray with a kettle and Ryan made us both some hot chocolate before we went to bed."

"Wow...it sounds like you're having a great time," Shenna laughs, pleased that Neirin is enjoying the proceedings. "Did you go to bed nicely?"

A moment of hesitation is followed by a cautious confession. "Well...we did stay up a bit...but Ryan said it was ok and I got up alright this morning without being grumpy," he adds hopefully.

"That's ok then," Shenna assures him. "Give Ryan a big hug from me, I miss you both so much."

"Muuum," Neirin cringes over the phone, "do I

have to...boys don't do that," he adds in a very grown up voice.

"I'm sure he'd appreciate it – this is a big day for Ryan and I think he'll need a hug," she tells him softly. "After all, he isn't just marrying me; he's going to be your dad too."

"Yeah," Neirin sounds happy and excited again, "it'll be for real...so that's alright then," he concludes brightly.

In plain clothes, Officer Palmer drives Shenna and Beccy to the church in Ryan's car. As well as the usual wedding nerves there is a palpable tension among those present when the bride arrives.

Standing in the lovely stone vestibule, Beccy stands beside Shenna as she smoothes the ivory silk of her ankle length dress and makes the matching shrug jacket more comfortable on her shoulders.

Holding a small posy of yellow and white roses with trailing ribbons intertwined Shenna moves up the isle with Neirin at her side. He is acting not only as her escort but also as Ryan's best man. They both wanted him to play an integral part in the service and for Neirin to feel that this was as much his day as theirs.

She hasn't seen their suits before and feels her

eyes become moist as she looks down at her little man.

Holding hands the music begins and they slowly make their way up the short aisle to where Ryan and the vicar are waiting. Only a handful of people have been invited, Shenna doesn't have any close living relatives and Ryan hasn't had contact with his mother for years.

It isn't until she is within two feet of Ryan that Shenna sees Felicity sitting next to Sadie and Roz. Her heart gives a strange twist, though the woman is smiling brightly enough, apparently happy for them on their wedding day – a far cry from the spiteful words she had thrown at Shenna not so long ago and at Ryan before he had thrown her off the dig.

What is she doing here? Did Ryan invite her...surely he would have told me?

Looking back at Ryan all thought of Felicity is forgotten. He stands tall and handsome, his blonde hair shorter than when last she saw him though not as short as when first they met.

He'd done that for her, she knew. She had told him that she liked his hair longer and he had obviously remembered that.

"You look beautiful," he whispers as he kisses her

cheek and takes her hand from Neirin. Ryan takes Neirin's hand and moves the boy to stand at his other side and gives it a squeeze as he glances down to wink at him.

Neirin smiles up, his brown eyes filled with love and joy and Ryan feels so proud.

The service is short but deeply moving, as all the guests agree afterwards. The photographer takes a few more photos, some in the church with the vicar and some in the lovely grounds.

Going back to the hotel where Ryan and Neirin spent the previous night, they are shown into a private room off the restaurant where an intimate wedding supper awaits them. They all fit around a large square of tables with Ryan, Shenna and Neirin sitting along the top.

Ryan stands to give a brief speech, thanking everyone for coming and sharing in their special day. He praises Neirin for carrying out his duties so splendidly, and everyone applauds, then he thanks Officer Palmer who is sat next to Beccy for acting as Shenna's chauffer and for keeping her safe. Then he turns to Beccy, smiling fondly and with gratitude.

"For weeks now you've put your own life on hold to watch over Shenna and Neirin," he tells her, "and I can't thank you enough for being willing to do so. We've become so used to having you around we've come to think of you as family and we'll be sad when it's time for you to leave," Ryan smiles warmly and Beccy's eyes fill with emotion. "As you all know, these last weeks have been stressful and sometimes frightening," he looks down at Shenna, his expression adoring and filled with love, "but I believe we have grown stronger in the face of adversity and I couldn't be prouder of my beautiful wife. Please raise your glasses in a toast to Mrs Shenna Tempest..."

An echo of voices repeats the toast and champagne is drunk in Shenna's honour. Then the lone voice of Paul speaks out, "To the bride and groom," and again the gathering raises their glasses repeating the toast and Ryan gives a nod of thanks to Paul.

Neirin goes home with Gail and her family, and at Shenna's insistence the two detectives in the patrol car now sit outside of their house for the night.

Beccy has a room of her own in the hotel, paid for by Ryan and along the same corridor as the bridal suite.

"Are you disappointed at having such a small

wedding," Ryan asks, holding Shenna to him in the privacy of their room.

"It was a lovely wedding, perfect for us no matter what." Her arms twine about his neck, her fingers enjoying the feel of his hair. "And I love my new name – Mrs Shenna Tempest," she tries the name out with a grin then kisses him soundly on the lips. Your wife...it's real and it's wonderful.

Easing the zip of Shenna's dress down her back, Ryan watches it slide down her body to puddle at her feet. "As ever, Mrs Tempest, you look sexy as hell when you're half dressed."

Shenna is still wearing the tiny silk shrug jacket and eases it off her shoulders and lets it fall to the floor with the strapless dress.

Ryan takes a step back to appreciate the view. Shenna is now wearing only the underwear she bought especially for her wedding night, an ivy silk basque with matching briefs and stockings and three inch stiletto heels.

Mine...sexy and adorable...I'll never stop being amazed at how much I love you.

Shenna's insides quiver before Ryan even lays a hand on her; just his look of pure lust mixed with love is enough to make her damp.

Collecting Neirin from Gail's the next morning, Ryan and Shenna look forward to taking him home and settling down to family life. Nothing can shake them now, the wedding was wonderful and the future is an adventure they can enjoy traversing together.

"We'll have a late honeymoon as soon as possible," Ryan promises. "I'll have to get someone to cover for me on the dig but it shouldn't take longer than a month or so to organise." *Less if I have my way!*

Putting a hand on his knee, Shenna looks over at Ryan in a state of bliss. "It isn't a problem," she tells him, "we have a lifetime of holidays to take and memories to collect." *A lifetime of love and happiness with Ryan Tempest, my wonderful husband!*

Covering her hand with his, Ryan feels like the luckiest man on the planet. "You're a very understanding woman, Mrs Tempest – I'll try not to take advantage of that."

"Oh, I'll let you know if you do," she grins happily.

"Ah, and so it begins," Ryan declares dramatically, "the shackles are on and the chains are being rattled – I can see I'm going to have to watch myself in future."

Pulling up in front of Gail's house they give the detectives in the patrol car a wave as they pass by. The officer who drove Shenna and Beccy to the church, and who has been shadowing them from the hotel, now gives a peep on the horn of his car and takes Beccy to the cottage ahead of them.

"Mum! Dad!" Neirin calls out as they walk into the lounge behind Gail. Shenna bends to scoop him up and after squeezing the breath out of Neirin, passes him over to Ryan for another huge hug. "Are we going home now?" he asks excitedly.

"Hey," Gail rebukes him playfully, "it wasn't that bad staying with us was it?"

Shaking his head, Neirin has the grace to look shame faced. "I do like staying..."

Gail ruffles his hair and gives him a peck on the cheek. "I was only playing – of course you want to go home...just don't forget to come back and see us."

Pulling up in front of the cottage, Ryan is immediately concerned. Not only are Officer Palmer and Beccy standing outside the cottage, but an unfamiliar van is parked on the drive and its occupants are talking to Beccy.

As soon as she sees them, Beccy hurries over as Ryan steps out of the car leaving Shenna and Neirin inside.

"What's happened?" Ryan demands his body rigid and on full alert.

"You'd better come in, but I wouldn't advise that Neirin, or even Shenna, be allowed to see what's inside."

Beccy moves ahead of Ryan and asks him not to touch anything. Before entering the house she gives him a pair of protective disposable slip-ons to put over his shoes and a pair of latex gloves for his hands. Once she's donned her own protective gear, Beccy leads him through the front door and straight into the lounge which looks like a hoard of vandals has been let loose in it.

The word 'WHORE' has been spray painted in two feet high letters on the lounge wall in what appears to be the same red paint as was sprayed on Shenna's car in the car park a few days ago.

"Bloody hell!" Ryan is thoroughly shocked by the level of damage that someone has inflicted on Shenna's home. "This is beyond vandalism," he observes and sees Beccy nod in agreement. "This was done by the person who abducted her and it's another form of violence against her." Again Beccy nods in agreement. You bastard!

"I'm afraid we didn't have the manpower to watch the cottage as well as Neirin and yourselves – I'm so sorry..." Becky lifts her hands in despair as she looks around the ruined home that she had been sharing with them. "Will you go back to the hotel?"

"I don't know," Ryan pushes a hand back through his hair and scans the room. "Is it the same upstairs?" He watches Beccy nod and growls with frustration. "What the fuck does he want?! Shenna has never done anything to anyone...why is she being hounded like this?!"

Moving to close the gap between them, Beccy lays a comforting hand on his arm. "We'll find out, Ryan. What with the car and now this, and the evidence from the farmhouse...there has got to be something we can use – they've got to slip up sometime."

Returning to the car, Ryan climbs inside then turns in his seat to face Shenna and Neirin. "Neirin, you're a clever lad and I won't start our family life by lying to you," he looks at Shenna then back at Neirin. "Someone broke into the cottage and has made an almighty mess of it, so there's no way that we can stay there for at least a few days." Again he looks at

Shenna to gauge her reaction to the news, but she is holding up well and he gives her a smile of appreciation. "We have two choices, we can go back to the hotel and stay there until the cottage is put back to rights, or we could get another port-a-cabin delivered now that the burnt out one has been cleared away." Shenna and Neirin both look confused. "It would be ours to live in together – we could go shopping for inflatable mattresses and bedding, it would have its own chemical loo and basic washing facilities," he tells them.

Once Neirin understands the plan he is all for it. "Camping, right here at the dig," he exclaims with wide eyes that turn to his mum imploringly. "Please say we can mum, please..."

Two sets of male eyes are looking her way expectantly and when she smiles Neirin lets out a scream of delight.

"I'll get on the phone, don't worry Shenna we'll be quite comfortable and more importantly, we'll be safe," Ryan states with conviction.

It's still quite early, only nine-thirty, but everyone is hard at work when Ryan pulls his car up alongside his office on the dig.

Neirin races out to tell everyone that they are

going to be living on the dig now, and Ryan receives a few concerned looks.

Paul and Carl, Sadie and Roz, all move closer to hear the news.

"Someone broke into the cottage last night," he explains to the crew, "and unfortunately they caused a great deal of damage. I'm going to arrange for another large port-a-cabin to be delivered and we'll be living on site for the time being."

The crew look from one to the other then Sadie speaks up for them all. "We're so sorry this happened, but especially now," she tells them and the rest of the crew nod in agreement. "We sort of made you a wedding cake, even the fellas did their bit," Sadie smiles hesitantly, "but maybe you don't feel like celebrating after...well..."

But Shenna dismisses their worries with a radiant smile. "We couldn't feel more like celebrating, isn't that right?" she turns to Ryan then glances down at Neirin. "And we didn't have time to organise a wedding cake so yours will be even more special."

"It's all boxed up at the minute," Sadie grins with relief, "we were going to bring it up to the cottage later. Perhaps we could have it at tea-time after our main meal and we can take photos on our phones of the bride and groom cutting the cake."

The whole group erupt into laughter and the mood is immediately lifted. "I need to get on the phone to organise our new accommodation," he tells Shenna and gives a wink to Neirin before striding off to his office.

"Do you want to see what we've found since you were last here?" Sadie asks Neirin and receives a big grin and a nod in reply. "We'll watch him if you want to get a coffee or something with Ryan," she assures Shenna. "And the beefy guys are never far away – we've got four of them night and day," she tells her and jerks a thumb in the direction of a gorilla sized security guard.

"Ok, thank you," Shenna tells her then looks down at her son. "Be good and be careful," she reminds him then turns towards Ryan's office.

When she steps up into the office, Ryan is on the phone busy making sure their temporary home is delivered today and will be supplied with the essentials he's stipulated.

Moving past him, Shenna takes down a mug and pours herself a coffee from the filter jug after checking that Ryan already has one.

Sitting across the desk from him she looks around

her and begins to read various notes and small posters that are stuck to the walls. Then she hears Ryan mention an obscene amount of money and swivels to look at him in horror.

"That's fine, yes, just make sure it gets here by five latest, it'll take time to set up and I have a five year old to think about."

When he puts his phone down Ryan looks warily at Shenna, not sure what has apparently upset her or if he's in trouble. This marriage thing is going to take some working out – are we about to have our first row?

"What!" he asks when she continues to gape at him? "I don't know the rules here Shenna, if you're mad at me for something you should just spit it out – I have no clue what I just did to upset you."

Giving her head a shake to clear it, Shenna gives a wan smile. "You haven't upset me, I just...I just...what was all that money for, it sounded like you were paying someone a small fortune for something."

"Oh that!" he dismisses out of hand and leans back in his chair somewhat relieved. "It was just the new living accommodation and a few supplies – we don't need to go shopping for bedding, or anything else, when I explained the situation they were more than happy to get what we need and deliver it at the same time."

"I'll just bet they were!" Crikey...you could buy a small house for not much more!

"You didn't marry a poor man, Shenna," Ryan is still unsure of his footing and feels like he's walking on shaky ground. "I told you I'd take care of you both and I will."

Getting up, Shenna rounds his desk and plonks herself down on his knees. Putting an arm around his neck she kisses him and only succeeds in confusing him further.

When he frowns she laughs, when his frown deepens Shenna giggles delightedly.

"I'm not mad at you...a little shocked maybe, but not mad." When she places a tender hand on his cheek he turns his head into her palm and kisses it. "As long as we have you the money doesn't matter, you're the most important part of our lives now – don't you know that? Don't you believe that?"

He feels almost hypnotised by her pixie green eyes. She is the loveliest creature he has ever known; that she loves him is a miracle he isn't sure he'll ever be able to believe completely.

"I don't know about love the way you do," Ryan tries to explain. "I know that I love you, that I love Neirin too, but I'm not sure how to express it or to accept it when it's offered – you might regret marrying an emotional cripple."

Taking his face between both her hands she looks deep into Ryan's troubled eyes. "There will be no regrets, and if I have to tell you every minute of every day that I love you so that you'll believe it, then that's just what I'll do," she declares firmly. "There are no emotional cripples in this relationship, just a couple getting to know each other and making adjustments until the fit is exactly right."

"You astound me," Ryan pulls her to him and wraps her in his love.

CHAPTER FOURTEEN

When the 'living accommodation' arrives, Shenna is stunned by the luxurious ten birth caravan.

It takes a lot of manoeuvering as Ryan realised it couldn't go in the same place as the burned out port-a-cabin they'd cleared away, as that is where Roz found the coins.

"Thank you," he tells the driver and his mate, "that was exceptional service and took a lot of effort – we appreciate it," and he hands them both a very generous tip.

Holding the keys between his thumb and forefinger, Ryan rattles them invitingly. "Anyone want to take a look?"

The crew hold back letting Ryan, Shenna and Neirin inspect their new home first.

"Oh boy," Neirin yells from a nearby bedroom, "we've all got our own rooms."

Shenna blushes and Ryan laughs. "Actually we'll have a spare," Ryan corrects and walks to the double bedroom at the back. "Your mum and I will be in here, which means you get to pick one of the other two."

"This one's got bunk-beds," Neirin puts his head out the door and smiles up at his mum and dad, "I could sleep on the top bunk and keep my books and things on the bottom."

"Sounds good," Shenna agrees, "we'll try to get some of your things later today." It'll help for you to have a few familiar things around you. They couldn't have ruined everything...could they?

"When I looked at this online," Ryan tells them as they continue their exploration, "I was really impressed with the lounge and kitchen – there's a lot of hidden storage so we shouldn't be swamped by our belongings."

"This is wonderful, Ryan," Shenna smiles and turns around on the spot with Neirin in her arms making him giggle. "Let's get the others in; I'll be able to cook us a proper meal, all of us together this evening."

Neirin runs to the door and shouts over to the waiting crew. "Come on in, mum's going to cook dinner for everyone," he tells them.

"There's no backing out now," Ryan chuckles and puts an arm round Shenna's shoulders.

Showing everyone around, Neirin takes them first to the bedroom he's chosen and enthuses over the bunk-beds, "And this one is mum and dad's room, it has a really big bed," he observes innocently.

"It's great," Sadie agrees, as they all make their way through the galley kitchen to the lounge area. "Crikey, caravans have changed since I stayed in one at Great Yarmouth as a kid," she tells Shenna and takes a seat opposite.

"Hey, you've got a TV," Paul comments excitedly, and gives Ryan a huge grin, "there's some big matches coming up in a couple of days – how do you feel about a lads night in?"

"Whoa, you're kicking me out before I've even got in," Shenna protests, then reconsiders. "Actually, I'm sure us girls could come up with an alternative girls night," she looks from Sadie to Roz with a raised brow, "something like a wine tasting night...maybe?"

"Yeah, and we could sample a few take-away

dishes; there's a great Chinese not too far away," Roz chimes in, "and they deliver within five miles."

With a deep chuckle and while affectionately rubbing Shenna's back, Ryan goes along with the jovial atmosphere. "I'll stand for the beer and a selection of wine for you ladies to sample," he tells them.

"Yes!" Paul punches the air and Carl joins in the general laughter.

"Hello..." a male voice calls through the open caravan door at the same time as knocking on it, "...Mrs Williams...could I have a word please."

Shenna turns to Ryan and everyone falls silent, including Neirin when he senses the change in atmosphere.

"That would be Mrs Tempest," Ryan corrects Detective Brent as he crosses to the door. "Please come in, Detective, I'll ask everyone to leave while we discuss...matters," he finishes cautiously.

The crew have already taken the hint and are ready to leave. "If you could set Neirin to work, I know he's been dying to get his hands mucky again," Shenna tells Sadie and receives a knowing nod by way of reply.

"Apologies for the slip," Detective Brent offers

Ryan his hand and then Shenna, "congratulations on your marriage – I'm sorry the homecoming was so upsetting."

"I...haven't actually seen it," Shenna admits. "Ryan went in with Beccy while Neirin and I stayed in the car."

Nodding his approval the detective takes a seat when Ryan waves a hand to indicate he should do so. "I don't think there would be anything gained from putting yourself through that kind of stress – Mr Tempest was able to help with most of the immediate questions we needed answering."

"And now," Ryan asks, "do you have more questions – or perhaps you have some good news for us." Christ we could do with some!

"A bit of both, I believe," Detective Brent answers cryptically. "It was noted that Miss Felicity Mayfield attended your wedding, yesterday. Would you mind telling me which of you invited the young woman?"

Shenna looks to Ryan and, like the detective, awaits his explanation. "It was a last minute thing," he groans and sighs, "she telephoned me at the hotel on my mobile – Felicity read the announcement in one of the broadsheets while she was in London." Getting up he strides up and down the lounge and kitchen, "She wanted to wish us well, to draw a line under the bad feeling and put it all behind us – are you seriously telling me that Felicity had something to do with what's been going on," he asks incredulous.

Moving to sit beside Shenna, Ryan takes her hand, "I thought it would help our future if we could put the recent past behind us."

He wasn't referring to anything that had happened to her, she knew, but Shenna finds herself unable to be quite so forgiving. "Felicity made her feelings plain, I don't believe they have changed," she states uncompromisingly.

"If you wouldn't mind, I'd like to hear in more detail exactly what Felicity Mayfield said to you and when," Detective Brent put in.

Going back to the moment when Felicity had introduced herself in a pretence of apologising for the noise from the dig site, Shenna tells of Felicity's jealously, of her intimidating behaviour and her unnatural anger over her relationship with Ryan.

Shaking her head, Shenna looks up at Ryan by her side, "It never occurred to me...I mean, she said she loved you...It couldn't have been Felicity," Shenna turns to the detective. "The attacker struck

Ryan... Felicity loved him, she wouldn't have hurt you like that," she finishes turning to lift confused eyes to her new husband.

Bringing a hand up to touch her face, Ryan wishes he could agree, "I was a fool not to think of her," he admits. "Her temper has grown vicious over the years, Felicity wants what she wants and not much stands in the way of her getting it."

"There is no doubt, I'm afraid," Detective Brent confirms, "we got a positive match on fingerprints – a substantial partial from one of the batteries in the voice altering device that we found in the farmhouse, and a whole host of others from the frenzied vandalism that occurred while you were at the hotel after your wedding." Rising to his feet, Detective Brent stands looking down at them both. "Felicity Mayfield is on the run, she left her hotel in a hurry but we'll find her – have no doubt about that!"

"So this is entirely my fault," Ryan reasons guiltily. "Felicity would never have harmed you if I had behaved better towards her." I should have known...should have seen the extent of her anger. And I was the one who triggered it! Me! Damn it!

"You can't know that," Shenna protests, "and it's not like you treated her badly. You told me you always made it clear that you were not the marrying kind, that yours was an adult consensual relationship that she enjoyed as much as you."

"Maybe I was fooling myself – taking what I wanted while giving nothing back." Ryan begins the process of self doubt and recrimination. "I should have ended it long ago instead of letting it drag on, maybe feeding her hope that I could give her more." Fool!

"This has to stop!" Getting to her feet Shenna moves to stand beside the detective. "Felicity was a real piece of work, which was down to her and not anything that you did or didn't do." Ryan doesn't look convinced. "Isn't that true...?" She demands of the detective.

"I'm not in any position to make judgements about your relationship with Miss Mayfield," the detective addresses Ryan. "But what I will say is, you need to call us if Felicity Mayfield makes contact with you again...she is a very dangerous woman!"

"Y.you...you don't have her," Shenna can hardly get her breath. "Neirin!" Dashing to the caravan door her eyes search the dig site for him. "Neirin!" she screams out and almost faints with relief when he comes out of the girls' port-a-cabin with Sadie on his heels.

Jumping down the step Shenna runs across the dig and sweeps her son into her arms. The security guards all come running and Ryan and Detective Brent are hard on her heels.

A shot rings out and the world stops...except for the movement of Shenna and Neirin falling in a heap to the ground.

"Nooooo!" Ryan's cry from the heart is gut-wrenchingly painful to hear. His eyes are open and he knows he's awake, but the scene that is unfolding before him is worse than any nightmare he could ever dream up. His new wife and son have been shot. My fault! My fault! My fault! Oh God help me, it's all my fault!

Felicity is captured and disarmed by two of the security guards after Roz rugby tackled her and brought her down. Screaming obscenities and clawing at her captors, Felicity is lead away. When Ryan reaches Shenna and Neirin he is relieved to see them both still breathing. Shenna is clutching Neirin tightly to her, shielding his body with her own.

"Is she gone, did they catch her?" Shenna's green eyes are wide with alarm and searching the near vicinity.

His hands and eyes search for injuries after Ryan

drops to his knees beside his family. "Are you hurt? Did she hit you?" I can't see any blood...no blood...and they're alive – thank God!

Shenna and Ryan just look at each other neither of them answering the other's questions.

"Muuuuum, you're squashing me!" Neirin tries to squirm out of her arms and instead finds himself and his mum in Ryan's all-encompassing embrace.

"Thank God you're both safe – I'd never forgive myself if she'd hurt either of you," Ryan states fervently.

That night's meal turns into an all-out celebration. Shenna cooks and the crew bring over the special wedding cake they made between them - even Neirin is allowed to stay up late.

Tucking him in later that evening, Shenna asks Neirin if he's alright about what happened today. "It's ok to feel worried or frightened, and if you need to talk, either me or Ryan will be happy to discuss it as best we can."

"It was scary," Neirin admits, and pulls his duvet up under his chin. "Did they really lock her up so she can't hurt us anymore?"

"Yes, they did," Shenna confirms quietly. "Some people get so angry that they lose the ability to reason, and Felicity was very angry."

"But why was she angry at us, we didn't do anything to Felicity?"

"No, you're right – but Felicity was very jealous because she wanted to be Ryan's wife and he didn't choose her." Shenna grimaces at the thought then turns it into a smile. "He chose us instead."

"I thought we were going to call him dad, now," Neirin frowns, more concerned with that than any ongoing doubts about Felicity.

Raising her eyebrows in surprise, Shenna gives a little laugh, "You are absolutely right," she admits. "But give me a break, I have to get used to it too – I bet even you will slip up sometimes."

But Neirin shakes his head firmly. "No, I won't, because he is my dad now, and I love him very much."

Giving him a cuddle, Shenna feels her eyes fill and has to swallow back the tears. "I love him very much too, and I know that he loves you right back."

CHAPTER FIFTEEN

The next couple of weeks are full and exciting, and everyone soon gets over the shock of Felicity's arrest. The cottage is almost ready to move back into, Ryan has paid a company well to make the job a priority. Now it is decorated and most of the new furniture has been delivered.

The coins that Roz found, in the wake of the burned out port-a-cabin being removed, have indeed turn out to be gold and exactly as Ryan described.

"We're going to have a display of our local finds in the County Hall, with lots of security to make sure none of the valuable artefacts go missing," Ryan briefs the team in his office. "Roz will be credited with finding the gold coins," and Ryan leads the crew in giving her a round of applause.

Blushing wildly, Roz covers her face with her hands then gives a shy smile and mouths the words 'thank you' to Ryan.

"You deserve it," Ryan smiles brightly making his blue eyes twinkle. Turning to look at them all one by one, including Shenna and Neirin, Ryan's smile slips and he looks a little sad. "I'm going to miss you all when we leave, which Shenna, Neirin and I will be doing in just over a month's time. It's always sad to move on when you've worked with such a great crew – I wish you all the very best of luck in making it in your chosen careers."

"But surely," Roz gasps and pales, "there could be more finds, more coins..."

Ryan shakes his head, "The dig will continue, but I won't be heading it up."

"We're moving to Egypt for a while," Shenna puts in. "We're not selling the cottage in case we want to come back, but we will be gone for at least a year."

Even Carl and Paul are devastated by the news. "I don't blame you guys for wanting to get away for a bit, after everything that's happened here," Paul tries to be reasonable, "but it won't be the same with someone else in charge."

"I've already arranged for Mitch Lawson to take over – he's experienced and a nice chap to boot." Ryan purses his lips and frowns. "I have to put my family first; Shenna and Neirin need to get away from here for a while."

"Well, at least we enjoyed it while it lasted," Sadie decides to brighten the mood. "And who knows, this Mitch guy might turn out to be even better than Ryan," she adds with a grin and steps smartly out of his reach.

His batting hand having missed its target, Ryan just laughs and points a finger at Sadie, "Cheeky madam, I'll put you on kitchen duty for a week if I hear anymore!"

"Sorry," she tells him with a mischievous grin that belies her apology, "I just couldn't resist. But I do have a question about the exhibition – will it include the log and photos of the earlier finds that got destroyed?"

"Absolutely," Ryan nods. "That includes the pottery that you helped recover," he tells Neirin.

Smiling brightly, Neirin looks at Roz and says, "Don't be sad, we made new friends and you found some really important coins."

Reaching over to give his hair a friendly ruffle,

Roz returns his smile, "You're right, how about we try and find some more?"

Looking up at his mum and over at Ryan, Neirin's eyes plead for permission to go with Roz.

"Ok, but don't wander off," Shenna warns him. "Just stay with Roz."

Two days later Shenna and her family move back into the cottage.

"There's about another four boxes to come up," Sadie tells Shenna when she puts down a pile of towels and sheets on the new settee. "Paul and Carl are going to bring those, I said I'd stay and help out here if you want to put me to work."

"Gladly," Shenna smiles grateful for the offer, "as well as putting all this away I need to make the beds up."

"Ok, well I could go and do that," Sadie suggests. "You know where you want all this," she says, waving a hand at the pots and pans, "making a bed up is pretty standard."

"Great, I've already put the sheets and quilts in the rooms," Shenna moves from the kitchen into the lounge and picks up a couple of pillows, "but you'll need to take these – anything else you need should be in the airing cupboard."

"Okey doke." Sadie takes the pillows and makes her way upstairs.

Looking around her, Shenna is thrilled to be moving back into the cottage. Even with the change in decor it is home. She's even gladder now that Ryan kept her and Neirin from seeing the mess someone had turned it into – she has enough bad memories without having to block those images out too.

Back at the dig site, Ryan is in his office finalising arrangements for his replacement and confirming that he will be joining an ongoing dig in Egypt after a couple of weeks of free time with his family.

"I'm looking forward to it," Ryan tells the organisers of the dig, then hangs up and goes out of his office to have a word with his crew.

Carl and Paul are on their way back from hauling the last of the boxes up to the cottage, and Roz is digging with Neirin at her side.

"If you could give me a minute," Ryan calls out to them and waits for them to form a small group, "I want to sort out the new living arrangements."

The group give a synchronised frown of confusion.

"New living arrangements...?" Paul asks.

"Yes, we now have a very comfortable caravan on

site," Ryan reminds them. "I had thought the girls might like to move in there and you lads move in to the girl's port-a-cabin."

"Won't the new guy expect to get the luxury caravan?" Carl asks sceptically.

"Mitch," Ryan deliberately uses his first name, "will be happy to use the office port-a-cabin's sleeping quarters just as we have. Believe me, that is luxury compared to some of the places we've had to sleep."

"Sounds good to me," Paul smiles enthusiastically, "there's more room in the girl's port-a-cabin anyway."

Turning to Roz, Ryan gives a smile that is full of praise, "You girls deserve a bit of pampering – you especially as you found the most valuable artefacts."

Blushing under his attentions, Roz is thrilled to know he appreciates her contribution to the dig. Looking up under her lashes, she says, "Thanks that means a lot."

"I'm getting hungry," Neirin looks up at Roz, "is it lunch time yet?"

"Just give me a minute and I'll take you up to your mum," Ryan tells him. "I'll bet she's already got some lunch ready for you."

"And you," Neirin smiles happily.

Giving a chuckle Ryan agrees, "I believe you might be right at that." This is going to take some getting used to, though I'm certainly not complaining.

Sadie is coming towards them as Ryan and Neirin make their way up to the cottage. "I was just coming to tell you that Shenna has your lunch ready," she chuckles "but it seems I'm not needed."

"Neirin's body clock already told him it's lunch time," Ryan smiles indulgently.

"I don't suppose the fellas have thought to put anything on for us yet?" she asks not hopeful in the slightest.

"I didn't notice anything like that going on – but maybe I'm wrong and they've prepared you a salad and sandwiches." Ryan gives her a wave as they walk on and Sadie just rolls her eyes.

Setting plates of sandwiches on the breakfast table in the kitchen, Shenna is humming to herself when Ryan and Neirin walk in.

"Well this is a scene of domestic bliss," Ryan states with a grin which Neirin joins in with.

"I'm so happy to be back home," Shenna tells them. "I've made ham sandwiches and a pot of tea, if anyone wants a yogurt for after's there's a selection in the fridge."

Halfway through their lunch, Ryan tells Shenna and Neirin about his conversation with Mitch Lawson, the archaeologist who is going to take over the dig after they leave.

"He's in Birmingham at the minute hosting his own exhibition - archaeology over the past ten years," Ryan explains. "He finished his last dig a couple of months ago and was asked to host the exhibition at the NEC in Birmingham for a couple of weeks. He's already been there for a week so wants to talk to me about this dig, where we are with it, the crew and the backers – just usual background stuff really."

"Will I get to meet him before we leave?" Neirin asks enthusiastically.

"Yes, you will – he'll want to have at least a day with me on site to handover and he may visit the site prior to that," he looks up at Shenna. "That's all part of what we need to discuss."

"And this discussion needs to take place in Birmingham?" she asks.

Ryan looks uncomfortable, "I haven't agreed to anything definite yet. I said I'd talk it over with you and let him know this afternoon."

"Then don't worry about us," and Shenna smiles over at Neirin, "we'll be fine, won't we?"

Neirin nods enthusiastically, "I'll look after mum," he says with a straight spine and serious eyes, "that's what dad told me to do."

"Good, that makes me feel a lot better," and he pats Neirin's shoulders with a firm hand. "Is this afternoon too soon?"

Pouring them all a cup of tea, Shenna shakes her head. "Actually, that fits around me perfectly – I still have a few boxes to sort through, new pots and other things to put away so I can get that out of the way while you're gone."

"Good, I'll give Mitch a ring and tell him to expect me – I can probably make it back for around midnight," he frowns, working out the travelling time and averaging the time he expects to spend with Mitch.

Looking worried, Shenna sips her tea and decides she can manage without Ryan for one night. "I'd rather you stayed overnight," she suggests. "These country roads can be treacherous at the best of times, late at night they are downright dangerous."

Nodding thoughtfully, Ryan eventually gives a rueful smile. "It probably would make more sense, but are you two sure you both feel ok about being here on your own?"

Shenna and Neirin look at each other and nod. "Felicity is behind bars, there's nothing for us to worry about," Shenna reaches over to place a reassuring hand over Ryan's, "except getting you safely back home. Travel back tomorrow and we'll be waiting for you – won't we?"

"Yep!" And Neirin giggles when Ryan reaches out and tickles his side.

"Ok, I'm convinced – overnight it is." Finishing his tea, Ryan excuses himself and goes off to make the call to Mitch.

"You could have a sleep over with Tommy or the twins," Shenna offers, concerned that Neirin might get frightened in the cottage without Ryan being there.

But Neirin shakes his head resolutely, "I can't look after you if I'm not here," he states logically, "and I told dad that I would."

"You don't need to worry about me, sweetheart, I'm a big girl and I can look after myself." Looking at her watch, Shenna tries to work out which of her friends to call.

"Ok, that's sorted," Ryan tells them when he

returns to the kitchen. "I'll leave in an hour and stay overnight at the same hotel as Mitch."

"If I give Juliette or Gail a call, would you mind dropping Neirin off for a sleepover on your way?" Without her car Shenna is seriously restricted in getting around. When Ryan nods, she turns to Neirin and asks him if he wants to stay with Tommy or the twins.

"But muuuum," Neirin tries to complain, but Shenna cuts him off.

"Neirin, I'm perfectly safe and so are you. I've stayed in this cottage on my own lots of times and you can't just stop going over to your friends because you're worrying about me...that wouldn't be right." And I want you to enjoy your friends before we have to leave them all behind us.

"Your mum's right," Ryan assures him, "Felicity is far away and can't hurt your mum anymore. Do you think I would leave if I thought she could?"

Looking uncertain, Neirin contemplates Ryan for a serious minute and then eventually smiles. "I suppose its ok," he gives in reluctantly. "May I go to the twins' house; I haven't had a sleepover there for ages?"

"I'll call Juliette and ask," Shenna promises.

"Now, if you've finished you can read for a while then I'll get an overnight bag packed for each of you."

"Dad," Neirin looks up at Ryan, "will you call to say goodnight?"

Ryan's heart misses a beat then floods with joy. "I'll go one better – if you chose a book I'll take it with me and read it to you over the phone before you go to sleep...how's that?"

With a grin a mile wide, Neirin jumps down and hugs Ryan around the legs. Looking at Shenna over the boys head, he struggles to cope with the generosity of Neirin's love.

"Ok, Neirin, your dad has to go back to the dig to tell everyone where he's going and he can't do that with you holding on to his legs," Shenna laughs and is overjoyed at the family scene.

An hour later and Shenna is on her own in the cottage for the first time since the whole Felicity nightmare was ended.

It's not like I'm not used to being on my own, I've done it hundreds of times. But I have to admit, it does feel a little bit creepy.

For the rest of that afternoon and into the evening, Shenna continues to put away all the new house contents that she has had to replace due to the vandalism and the last of the possessions they had with them in the caravan.

Crikey, I don't know how we found room for all this stuff in the caravan – I'm just glad we were only there for a short time.

At seven o'clock, Ryan calls to speak to her before calling to wish Neirin goodnight. "Are you ok," he asks Shenna, "I can still make it back by midnight if you'd rather?"

"No, that isn't necessary; I've got plenty to keep me busy here."

"Ok." The phone line goes quiet and Ryan has so much that he wants to say but isn't sure he knows how. "I want to tell you how much I miss you, yet that isn't really what I want to say at all," he tries to explain, his deep voice quiet and earnest. "I can say the words, Shenna, I can tell you that I love you but that still isn't what I want to say." Heaving a heavy sigh down the phone line, Ryan tries again. "I mean, I do love you but that isn't the half of it – I don't know how to express these feelings because I've never had them before...never believed in them before."

"Shh," Shenna hushes him gently, "you've shown

me in a thousand different ways already how much you care for me. And I care for you just as deeply, and just as confoundedly. But it will come to us, Ryan. Just give it time and the words won't matter."

"But I want to be able to say them, to know the right words and to know that I mean them," he reasons. "That isn't too much to ask, is it?"

"I wish you were here – if you could see the smile you've put on my face you wouldn't doubt that you've already found the right words or that I've loved hearing them," she whispers softly.

For another moment the line goes silent, only this time it's because they are content in their love. "I'll be home soon," Ryan tells Shenna, "now I'd better ring our boy and read him his bedtime story."

"Ok, he'll no doubt have my mobile on his pillow waiting for it to ring," Shenna smiles. "He loves you too, Ryan."

"That's the miracle of children, isn't it - their ability to love with such open trust," he muses in amazement. "I won't let him down, Shenna. I'll be the best dad I can be for him."

When the ten o'clock news comes on, Shenna is barely awake half lying on the settee.

Frowning at her own slovenliness, Shenna sits

herself up then goes to the kitchen to pour a glass of white wine from the fridge.

Just one, madam, or you might get in the habit of drinking when you can't sleep. And why is it that you can't sleep? It's because you're a love-sick puppy whose feeling sorry for herself, that's why! Shame on you!

By midnight, one glass of wine has turned into two and Shenna has finally fallen asleep, but on the settee rather than in her big empty bed.

"What...what was that?" Sitting up abruptly, Shenna tries to pull herself from sleep in order to make out what the noise is.

Then it comes again and she realises that someone is at the front door. Looking at the time she has to wonder who it can be and takes a look out of the front window before opening the door.

"Roz, is everything alright?" Shenna asks full of concern – no one, other than Ryan, has ever come from the dig to her cottage unless there was something wrong.

Holding up a plastic container, Roz gives a rueful half-smile, "I saw your light on, I hope you don't mind but I'm dying for a cup of tea and we're completely out of sugar – do you have some you could spare?"

With a little laugh, Shenna holds the door open. "Come on in, I've got plenty. Would you like me to make you a cup of tea now?"

"Only if you are going to have one, otherwise I can make one back at the dig," Roz offers politely.

When Shenna walks to the kitchen, Roz follows close behind and sits at the breakfast table.

"Aren't you scared being on your own here after what happened?" Roz asks, watching Shenna busy herself with the kettle and the teapot.

"No, this was my home long before it became the scene of a nightmare," Shenna replies almost convincingly. "I won't let anything tarnish the memories this place holds for me. I lived here with Cade, my first husband and the most loving man you could ever wish to meet. And now I live here with his son and another wonderful man who I've been lucky enough to meet."

Roz sits stonily watching the woman who stole her most precious love from her. "He loves me too, you know."

Shenna stops in the middle of pouring boiling water into the teapot. "I'm sorry...who loves you?" she asks believing she must still be half asleep.

"Ryan." Roz holds her chin up and dares Shenna

to deny it. "He's told me so. That's why he gave us the caravan – he said I deserved to be pampered; me especially as I'd found the most valuable artefacts on the dig."

"I'm sure Ryan is thrilled with your work – those coins alone will vindicate his belief in the site to uncover some significant Roman Britain history," Shenna tries to reason, unsure of the younger woman's disposition having never seen this side of Roz before.

With an expression turned cold and hard, Roz produces a carving knife and places it on the table in front of her.

"I know you tricked him," she tells Shenna, "that you lured him into bed with your 'woe is me' act." Roz' eyes have taken on a look that Shenna can only think of as insane. "Why couldn't you just leave – I gave you enough chances, enough warnings about what would happen if you didn't, but you just ignored me," Roz sneers. "Just like everyone else, you don't see me or listen to me unless you need me to do something for you. People like me don't exist in your bright shiny world!"

"It was you...?" Shenna is only now comprehending the danger she is in. "But I thought...Felicity..."

"Felicity!" Roz spits the name out with contempt. "She was just too easy – I used the batteries from her lady-shaver, vain bitch!" Roz' laughter frightens Shenna more than anything. "And the Cottage, well, I just played up to her in the church, by the time the photos were finished she was angry as hell – I knew that temper of hers would get her into trouble one day."

"What is it that you want, Roz? What exactly do you want me to do?"

"What I told you to do when I stuffed you into that river-bank," Roz gives Shenna a wicked smile, "die...just die and get out of my way."

With her heart pounding and trying not to stare at the large carving knife that she herself had bought several years previously and had recently left behind in the caravan, Shenna keeps her voice calm and reassuring. "I don't believe you really mean that, Roz. I've always valued you as a person, and so has Neirin," she emphasises gently. "And I know that Ryan thinks a great deal of you too...but he doesn't love you, Roz – he cares for you as a valued friend."

Shaking her head, Roz gives a sneering smile. "That's just what he wants you to think – you trapped him into marriage by using Neirin. He never would have married you but for him!"

"I'm sorry Roz...I can see that you care for Ryan a great deal...but he doesn't love you...not in the way you want him to," Shenna reiterates quietly, but firmly, determined not to play along with Roz' self-delusions.

"You're wrong," and now Roz not only looks insane but her eyes have filled with a determination that Shenna fears.

As Roz picks up the carving knife from the table, Shenna tries to stand her ground knowing that any form of retreat will only encourage pursuit.

"Roz, this isn't necessary – I can see that I've lost, but you have to give me time to leave, to pick up Neirin and take him far away," Shenna reasons quietly, without any threat in her voice.

Frowning, Roz hesitates and lays the knife back down on the table. "You'll leave...before Ryan gets back?" When Shenna nods, Roz begins to formulate a plan. "I'll stay here till morning then take you and your luggage over to get Neirin, then I'll drive you a long way off and you can make your own way to god-knows-where and I'll be rid of you!"

Laughing at her own brilliance, Roz stares at Shenna like she doesn't have a care in the world. "I don't know why I didn't just do this in the first place," she tells Shenna. "I'll take that tea now," and she waves a hand at the teapot on the work-surface to the side of Shenna.

Not daring to turn her back on Roz, Shenna moves mechanically to make two cups of tea then takes them over to the breakfast table.

"If I'd known how you felt about Ryan I would never have gotten in your way." Shenna tries to instigate a woman-to-woman friendly chatty atmosphere, "In fact, I feel pretty rotten for not realising – I'm sorry Roz."

"People like you are never really sorry," Roz doesn't smile or hide her contempt for Shenna. "You just set your mind on what you want and take it – you need to be able to see people to know how they feel – you've never seen me, and that's your mistake!"

She's right! How many times have I smiled and waved but not bothered to take the time to chat...even just a brief 'how are you doing' might have made Roz feel more accepted – instead of alienated...transparent and alone.

"You're right, I realise that now – but that's my loss, Roz, and my shame," Shenna admits looking Roz steadily in the eyes. "If I'd made more of an effort to get to know all of you, instead of continuing in my own little world, I'd have understood the boundaries and not trodden all over your feelings." For a second they just look at each other – Roz stunned by the seemingly sincere remorse and Shenna appalled at her own selfishness. "I'm sorry Roz...I truly am."

"So...you'll leave...no tricks...you won't come back?"

"No, I won't come back Roz," and she means it – if God will allow her to survive one last time she will take Neirin and leave her heart behind. But I'll always love you, Ryan. Always.

Just as Shenna thinks the worst is over, a movement catches her eye and she looks towards it before she can stop herself.

Roz immediately picks up the knife, sensing danger at her back. "Get in here, whoever you are," she demands and moves round the table, nearer to Shenna, "or I'll put this knife right through her. Now!"

"There's no need for that," Detective Brent's calm voice precedes him into the kitchen, "we heard it all, you weren't going to harm Mrs Tempest, you were going to give her a lift as I understood it."

Looking confused but still agitated, Roz continues to hold the knife to Shenna abdomen. "You didn't come here to arrest me?"

Eyebrows raised Detective Brent moves slowly further into the room. "Not at all – we came to tell Mrs Tempest that we have caught Felicity Mayfield's accomplice, one Max Gower," he tells Shenna, his eyes trying to convey reassurance. "He's a vagabond with just enough sense to get your abduction right then take you to the neighbouring farm, just as Felicity ordered and paid him to do," the detective lies.

"That's right! That's right!" Roz exclaims hardly believing her luck. The stuck up bitch is going to take the blame for all of it and I can just pick up where I left off – I'll have Ryan all to myself!

The man himself moves into the doorway, having driven at breakneck speed once Detective Brent had told him of the arrest of Gower and his confession to being paid by Roz to kidnap Shenna. "I'm here, Roz...we can go now, if you'd only told me how you felt you could have saved us both a lot of heartache."

Even Shenna had to look at Ryan carefully to ascertain that he was playing a role – he sounded so convincing, and Roz thought so too.

"You do love me!" Roz' ecstatic expression was hard to witness, so dazzled by Ryan's presence that she forgot the knife and let it fall unheeded to the kitchen floor.

With open arms, Ryan takes a step towards Roz and she races into them before he can take another – holding him, burying her face in his warmth, Roz doesn't see or hear or feel anything but Ryan, his heart thudding loud and strong as she clings to him.

His arms close around her and his voice soothes away the madness. "Come on, Roz, let's get out of here."

Detective Brent and Officer Becket have already moved back into the lounge and ordered the other officers to make themselves scarce while Ryan brings out the suspect.

Looking at Brent and Becket sat seemingly unconcerned on the settee, Roz moves with Ryan out of the house and down the garden path. When they reach the police cars out front, Ryan gives one of the officers a nod and he moves in quietly to handcuff Roz.

"But we're going home...we're going back to the dig...why are you letting them do this...?"

His anguish is deep and heartfelt. "It's alright,

Roz, I'll be right behind you in my car – we just need to straighten this out, then we can get on with our lives."

Uncertain and afraid, Roz gives a tremulous smile, "You'll be right behind me? You'll tell them it's ok now?"

Nodding, Ryan watches them load a scared but unprotesting Roz into the back of the patrol car.

EPILOGUE

Three years later

"Thea, are you listening," Neirin puts the bedtime storybook he is reading to his little sister down in his lap. "You chose this book."

"She loves that story," Shenna smiles over at her son, so tall and handsome, just like his father had been, "just give her something to play with, you know she likes to be doing something all the time."

Thea's green pixie eyes blink up at her big brother adoringly, her titian curls framing her lovely face. "Peas." With her arm held out in the direction of her toy-box, Thea opens and closes her little fist in a 'gimmee' gesture, then repeats her version of please.

"You stay there, I'll get her a little toy then she'll

settle down."

Shenna bends to the toy-box and fishes out a little finger toy that has beads to turn and move along thick wires. Standing up, Shenna passes the toy to Thea and gets a beaming smile for her trouble.

"Are you alright, mum?" Neirin asks when she presses a hand to the small of her back and arches it to stretch out a few kinks.

"I'm fine, I don't remember getting this type of back pain with you or Thea, it's just a niggle, nothing to worry about," Shenna smiles over at her children, loving how close they are.

Neirin has always been a caring child, but since Thea was born he's been a doting big brother. With another baby due any day now, Shenna is glad that Neirin likes to help put Thea to bed.

"I'll be back up to kiss Thea goodnight," she tells him, "I just need to sit down for a bit."

Ryan watches his wife walk down the stairs into the open lounge. "You look lovely," he smiles adoringly, "but tired, if you don't mind me saying."

Sitting down next to him on the settee, Shenna shakes her head and rubs loving hands over her enormous stomach. "Lovely is not a word that comes to mind when I see myself in a mirror these days," she protests. "But actually, I do love being pregnant – though I shan't miss him playing football with my bladder!"

"Him...you seem to be favouring a boy this time," Ryan notes and puts his hand on her stomach to feel his child kick."

"Mmm, I don't know why I keep saying that," she tells Ryan, "it isn't like I peeked at the ultrasound."

Just as they did with Thea, Shenna and Ryan have decided from the outset not to find out the sex of the baby and so they've chosen both a boys and a girl's name to cover both eventualities.

"I think Scot wants out," Ryan laughs as the baby gives an almighty kick.

"Well Scot or Emily will just have to wait," Shenna talks directly to her baby bump. "It's your sister's birthday tomorrow so we'll have no hospital dashes in the middle of the party, if you please!"

"Have you heard from Sadie and the rest?" Ryan grins at the picture in his mind that Shenna's plea puts there.

"Yes, they're all coming." Then she smiles at him with a coy sidelong look.

"What? You look like someone who's keeping a secret – give," he tells her with a mock firm look.

Shenna smiles happily "Sadie and Carl have gotten engaged – he was always soft on her but he was a bit slow to show it back at the dig."

"That seems like a long time ago, doesn't it?" Ryan sighs and frowns at the memory. "And yet it also seems like five minutes ago, too." I still wake in the night and have to check that you're safe and sound by my side.

"Stop dwelling on the negatives – that was a lovely part of our lives," Shenna touches his cheek to turn his face to look at her, "and from what we've found out, Roz is doing well."

"I don't mind paying for her care – I'm happy to do that for someone who used to be a friend," Ryan states cautiously, "but I would never want her to be part of our lives...ever. I could never trust her again...not with you and definitely not with our children!"

"It's ok," Shenna's voice is soft and loving, "we don't have to be in contact with Roz directly – we've managed to stay up to date with her progress and the doctors agreed not to tell her that you are picking up the bills, so she has no reason to get in touch when she eventually does get out." But I couldn't agree more; I wouldn't want Roz anywhere near our family...not ever!

Although Felicity was given twelve months in gaol for the vandalism to the cottage, she got out after six months with good behaviour. Apparently Roz had been subtly goading her the whole time, something she'd been good at – dropping a hint here, a nudge of encouragement there, and all the while feeding Felicity's jealousy of Shenna. It had also been Roz that shot at Shenna at the dig, then squeezed the gun into the hand of a, by then, delirious Felicity when she brought her down.

Nodding, Ryan decides to let the subject drop, but determines to keep an eye on the situation. "So who is definitely coming tomorrow?"

"Juliette and the twins are coming, though her husband works shifts and won't be able to make it. Gail and Terry are both coming and bringing Tommy. Then there's Carl, Sadie and Paul and a bunch of toddlers from the playgroup Thea attends, and a couple of Neirin's new friends, so he doesn't feel left out."

With a look of suppressed horror, Ryan tries to smile. "That's quite a houseful," he states unconvincingly. "Are you sure you're up to it?"

Sitting forward, Shenna asks Ryan to rub the bottom of her spine, it really is giving her gip. "I don't remember getting this with the others," she moans with pleasure as Ryan's large hands massage the nagging ache. "It's like a toothache, persistent and impossible to ignore."

"I'm sure everyone would understand if you cancelled the party," Ryan suggests.

"Thea would mind," Shenna turns to look at him with a frown. "You're just worried about all those toddlers, but you needn't, their mum's will be staying with them so it won't be so bad."

"Their mum's too, are you sure the house won't split at the seams!" Ryan has no idea what to expect; Thea's first birthday had been spent quietly with just them and the dig crew coming for a birthday tea. This sounds way beyond anything he knows how to handle.

"I'd better go back up," Shenna stands and flashes Ryan a reassuring smile before making her way up to Thea's bedroom.

Listening at the door she can hear Neirin pointing at interesting pictures and telling Thea what they're all about.

"I've come for my kisses," Shenna tells them, as she walks in the room. Thea immediately flings out her arms and Neirin laughs, having to duck out of the way. "Hey, mind your brother," Shenna sits on the bed and cuddles with Thea. Although she will only be two tomorrow, she is already out of nappies day and night and Shenna is trialling her in a bed with the cot sides removed.

So far it has worked well, and as Thea likes her sleep she doesn't get up too early, usually toddling into her mum and dad's room around six.

"Ok, night-night," and Shenna gives her daughter a kiss then tucks her in along with Dillon, her stuffed rabbit who goes wherever Thea goes.

The party is busy and noisy, and Ryan tries to stay on the sidelines. I don't know how they do it...how do kids manage to miss their mouths so much...there's as much food on their clothes as in their stomachs. But...they seem to be enjoying themselves.

"Mr..." a hand tugs at his trousers and a head of blond curls and blue innocent eyes looks up at him, "...I don't got no juice."

Before Ryan can answer a stern looking woman wags a finger at the boy and Ryan is reminded of his mother.

"Sam Baylis, you have better manners than that," she frowns at the boy, then smiles indulgently and sets Ryan's protective instincts at ease. "What's the magic word?"

Holding his plastic beaker up to Ryan, Sam says, "Please."

"Well said, young man," and Ryan ruffles Sam's curls. "Let's see what we can find in the kitchen," and picks the boy up without a care for his sticky fingers.

"Fatherhood suits you," Sadie tells him when he walks in still carrying Sam. "What can I get you – I'm on kitchen duty, though really…I'm just glad to be out of the way, I've never seen so many kids!"

Giving a sympathetic laugh, Ryan nods in agreement. "This one 'don't got no juice'," he tells Sadie using Sam's own words.

"Well we can certainly do something about that," and she takes the cup that the little boy holds out to her. "We have orange, blackberry and apple or just straight apple juice," she tells Sam who gives the list some consideration.

"Apple," he states, then adds, "please," when Ryan gives him a frown like the one the boy's mum had given him.

"Hey, you speak kiddie-lingo," Sadie congratulates Ryan when he sets the boy down to let him get back to the party. "I thought only mummies were able to use the evil eye – you're a natural!"

"I just copied what his mother did," Ryan laughs, feeling quite proud of himself, "but it did work rather well, didn't it – I'll have to remember that one with Thea."

A bustle of women sounds outside the kitchen where Ryan and Sadie frown with curiosity at each other. Then they hear someone say, "Just breathe, let's get you sat down and someone will find your husband."

"Holy shit! It must be the baby!" Ryan has paled and Sadie stares at him in shock.

"Is Shenna due today?" Sadie asks, and then shakes her head, "No, no, I'm sure Shenna said she has another three weeks to go – this can't be right!"

They both move at the same time, following the crowd which has gathered in the lounge.

"Oh, here he is now," one of the mums hovering over Shenna smiles. "We'll get out of your way; just let us know if there's anything we can do to help." Then she waves everyone out of the room.

"I'm fine," Shenna tries to stand but Ryan pushes her gently back into the armchair. "I can do this – I just want Thea to have her party then we can go to the hospital."

With a suspicious frown, Ryan asks her, "Just how long have you been having contractions?" He remembers the panic he'd felt when she'd gone into labour with Thea, this time he is determined to do it right. "We are not doing a last minute dash like we did last time...how long, Shenna?"

"I think it's been starting slowly over the last couple of days..." She watches Ryan pale drastically and his mouth just falls open wordlessly. "It isn't as bad as you think...it was just back pain but then it seemed to move round to the front this morning and now it's...aaaaahhhhh!" Clutching her stomach, Shenna tries to breathe through a strong contraction.

Sadie looks across at Ryan above Shenna's head. "You need to go," she mouths in a whisper, and Ryan nods in agreement.

"I'll make sure Thea enjoys her party," Sadie offers bravely. "You get to the hospital and Neirin will help me to look after Thea. The clown is due to arrive any minute so the little darlings will be nicely entertained," Sadie tells her, praying that it will be that easy.

"Are you sure?" Shenna takes in a deep breath then lets it out slowly. "I could probably manage another couple of hours..."

"Not on your life!" Ryan gets to his feet and glowers down at his wife. "I'm getting your suitcase then we are going, you can phone the kids once it's all over." He turns to Sadie, "Can you stay the night if I don't make it back?"

"No problem, now go and let me know how things progress."

The drive to the hospital is tense. Shenna's contractions have dropped to less than two minutes apart and are very strong.

"Ok, just do what the midwife told you – breathe through the pain and try to focus on something nice," Ryan tries to calm Shenna and himself at the same time. "Bloody hell, we missed the lights!"

As they sit in traffic waiting for the lights to change, Shenna gives a loud cry that even startles the people in the car next to them.

"I need to push," she gasps while trying to stop her body from doing what it naturally wants to do.

"Oh, Jesus," Ryan wipes the back of his hand over his damp forehead. "You can't have that baby in the car...cross your legs or something," he begs then lets out a relieved oath when the lights finally change. "Five minutes...just hold on tight for five minutes." This can't be happening...not again...and definitely not in the car!

Shenna is breathing through another strong contraction when Ryan pulls up outside the private maternity hospital. He'd spent weeks during her first pregnancy scoping out the ones that came highly recommended and had even paid them a visit in person before Shenna had started her antenatal appointments.

Now he has every confidence in the hospital but needs to get her inside safely before they can do their jobs.

Dashing into reception he quickly tells them the situation and a small group of staff follow him out to the car with a wheelchair.

Even when they are on their way to the labour ward, Ryan feels like pulling his hair out when Shenna's pain reaches a new high.

"Ok, Shenna, let's get you onto the bed and see what's happening," a lovely young midwife, who Ryan thinks can't long have left school, encourages Shenna quietly.

Once on the bed, the midwife examines Shenna then declares her ready to push.

Ryan sits nervously by Shenna's head and strokes her damp hair back from her face. "You are so amazing, so wonderfully brave," then feels her squeeze the blood from his hand as another contraction hits and she starts to push.

The midwife tells her to pant through the next one then tells her that one more strong push should deliver the baby.

A loud cry of protest echoes in the room – baby Scot Tempest has made an entrance weighing in at eight pounds and fourteen ounces.

"Our son," Shenna kisses the baby's forehead then turns adoring eyes to Ryan. "We have a son," she tells him, the wonder of it all so vivid and apparent.

"We already have a son," Ryan states proudly, "now he has a little brother to go with his sister."

"I love you," Shenna puts a hand to Ryan's cheek. "You are the kindest man and best dad in the whole world."

"Hey, I even learned how to do a disapproving scowl that had Sam saying 'please' without me having to ask him," Ryan tells her proudly and gives her a demonstration. "I thought I might try it out on our two – it might only have worked because his mum had done it a few minutes before."

Shenna gives a big yawn and a low chuckle. "Sorry, I'm a bit worn out," she tells him as her eyes start to drift closed.

"Shenna...?"

"Mmm..."

"This is the last one...right?" His nerves have only just stopped jangling.

"What...? Oh, no..." she yawns and snuggles the baby into her arms, "...I've always wanted a big family...four or five at least." Then falls asleep leaving Ryan stunned and disbelieving.

"Now she tells me..."

*****

If you have enjoyed reading this book, please leave a review at the place of purchase.

9 781910 753033